The Complete

Sorceress of the Strand

The Complete

Sorceress of the Strand

by L. T. Meade

and Robert Eustace

First Beltham House Edition, 2008

Originally serialized in *The Strand Magazine*

October 1902 – March 1903

Published by London: Ward, Lock 1903

Also from Beltham House

Brotherhood of the Seven Kings by L.T. Meade & Robert Eustace

The Secret of the Night by Gaston Leroux

Fantomas of London by Marcel Allain

The Exploits of Juve by Marcel Allain & Pierre Souvestre

A Nest of Spies by Marcel Allain & Pierre Souvestre

A Royal Prisoner by Marcel Allain & Pierre Souvestre

Available on Amazon.com or www.lulu.com

I. Madame Sara

EVERYONE in trade and a good many who are not have heard of Werner's Agency, the Solvency Inquiry Agency for all British trade. Its business is to know the financial condition of all wholesale and retail firms, from Rothschild's to the smallest sweetstuff shop in Whitechapel. I do not say that every firm figures on its books, but by methods of secret inquiry it can discover the status of any firm or individual. It is the great safeguard to British trade and prevents much fraudulent dealing

Of this agency I, Dixon Druce, was appointed manager in 1890. Since then I have met queer people and seen strange sights, for men do curious things for money in this world.

It so happened that in June, 1899, my business took me to Madeira on an inquiry of some importance. I left the island on the 14th of the month by the *Norham Castle* for Southampton. I embarked after dinner. It was a lovely night, and the strains of the band in the public gardens of Funchal came floating across the star-powdered bay through the warm, balmy air. Then the engine bells rang to "Full speed ahead", and, flinging a farewell to the fairest island on earth, I turned to the smoking-room in order to light my cheroot.

"Do you want a match, sir?"

The voice came from a slender, young-looking man who stood near the taffrail. Before I could reply he had struck one and held it out to me.

"Excuse me," he said, as he tossed it overboard, "but surely I am addressing Mr. Dixon Druce?"

"You are, sir," I said, glancing keenly back at him, "but you have the advantage of me."

"Don"t you know me?" he responded, "Jack Selby, Hayward's House, Harrow, 1879."

"By Jove! so it is," I cried.

Our hands met in a warm clasp, and a moment later I found myself sitting close to my old friend, who had fagged for me in the bygone days, and whom I had not seen from the moment when I said goodbye to the "Hill" in the grey mist of a December morning twenty years ago. He was a boy of fourteen then, but nevertheless I recognized him. His face was bronzed and good-looking, his features refined. As a boy Selby had been noted for his grace, his well-shaped head, his clean-cut features; these characteristics still were his, and although he was now slightly past his first youth he was decidedly handsome. He gave me a quick sketch of his history.

"My father left me plenty of money," he said, "and The Meadows, our old family place, is now mine. I have a taste for natural history; that taste took me two years ago to South America. I have had my share of strange adventures, and have collected valuable specimens and trophies. I am now on my way home from Para, on the Amazon, having come by a Booth boat to Madeira and changed there to the Castle Line.

But why all this talk about myself?" he added, bringing his deck chair a little nearer to mine. "What about your history, old chap? Are you settled down with a wife and kiddies of your own, or is that dream of your school days fulfilled, and are you the owner of the best private laboratory in London?"

"As to the laboratory," I said, with a smile, "you must come and see it. For the rest I am unmarried. Are you?"

"I was married the day before I left Para, and my wife is on board with me."

"Capital," I answered. "Let me hear all about it."

"You shall. Her maiden name was Dallas; Beatrice Dallas. She is just twenty now. Her father was an Englishman and her mother a Spaniard; neither parent is living. She has an elder sister, Edith, nearly thirty years of age, unmarried, who is on board with us. There is also a step-brother, considerably older than either Edith or Beatrice. I met my wife last year in Para, and at once fell in love. I am the happiest man on earth. It goes without saying that I think her beautiful, and she is also very well off. The story of her wealth is a curious one. Her uncle on the mother's side was an extremely wealthy Spaniard, who made an enormous fortune in Brazil out of diamonds and minerals; he owned several mines. But it is supposed that his wealth turned his brain. At any rate, it seems to have done so as far as the disposal of his money went. He divided the yearly profits and interest between his nephew and his two nieces, but declared that the property itself should never be split up. He has left the whole of it to that one of the three who should survive the others. A perfectly insane arrangement, but not, I believe, unprecedented in Brazil."

"Very insane," I echoed. "What was he worth?"

7

"Over two million sterling."

"By Jove!" I cried, "what a sum! But what about the half-brother?"

"He must be over forty years of age, and is evidently a bad lot. I have never seen him. His sisters won't speak to him or have anything to do with him. I understand that he is a great gambler; I am further told that he is at present in England, and, as there are certain technicalities to be gone through before the girls can fully enjoy their incomes, one of the first things I must do when I get home is to find him out. He has to sign certain papers, for we shan't be able to put things straight until we get his whereabouts. Some time ago my wife and Edith heard that he was ill, but dead or alive we must know all about him, and as quickly as possible."

I made no answer, and he continued:--

"I'll introduce you to my wife and sister-in-law tomorrow. Beatrice is quite a child compared to Edith, who acts towards her almost like a mother. Bee is a little beauty, so fresh and round and young-looking. But Edith is handsome, too, although I sometimes think she is as vain as a peacock. By the way, Druce, this brings me to another part of my story. The sisters have an acquaintance on board, one of the most remarkable women I have ever met. She goes by the name of Madame Sara, and knows London well. In fact, she confesses to having a shop in the Strand. What she has been doing in Brazil I do not know, for she keeps all her affairs strictly private. But you will be amazed when I tell you what her calling is."

"What?" I asked.

"A professional beautifier. She claims the privilege of restoring youth to those who consult her. She also declares

8

that she can make quite ugly people handsome. There is no doubt that she is very clever. She knows a little bit of everything, and has wonderful recipes with regard to medicines, surgery, and dentistry. She is a most lovely woman herself, very fair, with blue eyes, an innocent, childlike manner, and quantities of rippling gold hair. She openly confesses that she is very much older than she appears. She looks about five-and-twenty. She seems to have traveled all over the world, and says that by birth she is a mixture of Indian and Italian, her father having been Italian and her mother Indian. Accompanying her is an Arab, a handsome, picturesque sort of fellow, who gives her the most absolute devotion, and she is also bringing back to England two Brazilians from Para. This woman deals in all sorts of curious secrets, but principally in cosmetics. Her shop in the Strand could, I fancy, tell many a strange history. Her clients go to her there, and she does what is necessary for them. It is a fact that she occasionally performs small surgical operations, and there is not a dentist in London who can vie with her. She confesses quite naively that she holds some secrets for making false teeth cling to the palate that no one knows of. Edith Dallas is devoted to her--in fact, her adoration amounts to idolatry."

"You give a very brilliant account of this woman," I said. "You must introduce me tomorrow."

"I will," answered Jack with a smile. "I should like your opinion of her. I am right glad I have met you, Druce, it is like old times. When we get to London I mean to put up at my town house in Eaton Square for the remainder of the season. The Meadows shall be re-furnished, and Bee and I will take up our quarters some time in August; then you must come and see us. But I am afraid before I give myself up to mere pleasure I must find that precious brother-in-law, Henry Joachim Silva."

"If you have any difficulty apply to me," I said. "I can put at your disposal, in an unofficial way, of course, agents who would find almost any man in England, dead or alive."

I then proceeded to give Selby a short account of my own business.

"Thanks," he said presently, "that is capital. You are the very man we want."

The next morning after breakfast Jack introduced me to his wife and sister-in-law. They were both foreign-looking, but very handsome, and the wife in particular had a graceful and uncommon appearance.

We had been chatting about five minutes when I saw coming down the deck a slight, rather small woman, wearing a big sun hat.

"Ah, Madame," cried Selby, "here you are. I had the luck to meet an old friend on board--Mr. Dixon Druce--and I have been telling him all about you. I should like you to know each other. Druce, this lady is Madame Sara, of whom I have spoken to you, Mr. Dixon Druce--Madame Sara."

She bowed gracefully and then looked at me earnestly. I had seldom seen a more lovely woman. By her side both Mrs. Selby and her sister seemed to fade into insignificance. Her complexion was almost dazzlingly fair, her face refined in expression, her eyes penetrating, clever, and yet with the innocent, frank gaze of a child. Her dress was very simple; she looked altogether like a young, fresh, and natural girl.

As we sat chatting lightly and about commonplace topics, I instinctively felt that she took an interest in me even greater than might be expected upon an ordinary introduction. By slow degrees she so turned the conversation as to leave Selby and his wife and sister out, and then as they moved away she came a little nearer, and said in a low voice:

"I am very glad we have met, and yet how odd this meeting is! Was it really accidental?"

"I do not understand you," I answered.

"I know who you are," she said, lightly. "You are the manager of Werner's Agency; its business is to know the private affairs of those people who would rather keep their own secrets. Now, Mr. Druce, I am going to be absolutely frank with you. I own a small shop in the Strand--a perfumery shop--and behind those innocent-looking doors I conduct the business which brings me in gold of the realm. Have you, Mr. Druce, any objection to my continuing to make a livelihood in perfectly innocent ways?"

"None whatever," I answered. "You puzzle me by alluding to the subject."

"I want you to pay my shop a visit when you come to London. I have been away for three or four months. I do wonders for my clients, and they pay me largely for my services. I hold some perfectly innocent secrets which I cannot confide to anybody. I have obtained them partly from the Indians and partly from the natives of Brazil. I have lately been in Para to inquire into certain methods by which my trade can be improved."

"And your trade is----?" I said, looking at her with amusement and some surprise.

"I am a beautifier," she said, lightly. She looked at me with a smile. "You don't want me yet, Mr. Druce, but the time may come when even you will wish to keep back the infirmities years. In the meantime can you guess my age?"

"I will not hazard a guess," I answered.

"And I will not tell you. Let it remain a secret. Meanwhile understand that my calling is quite an open one, and I do hold secrets. I should advise you, Mr. Druce, even in your professional capacity, not to interfere with them."

The childlike expression faded from her face as she uttered the last words. There seemed to ring a sort of challenge in her tone. She turned away after a few moments and I rejoined my friends.

"You have been making acquaintance with Madame Sara, Mr. Druce," said Mrs. Selby. "Don't you think she is lovely?"

"She is one of the most beautiful women I have ever seen," I answered, "but there seems to be a mystery about her."

"Oh, indeed there is," said Edith Dallas, gravely.

"She asked me if I could guess her age," I continued. "I did not try, but surely she cannot be more than five-and-twenty."

"No one knows her age," said Mrs. Selby, "but I will tell you a curious fact, which, perhaps, you will not believe. She was bridesmaid at my mother's wedding thirty years ago. She declares that she never changes, and has no fear of old age."

"You mean that seriously?" I cried. "But surely it is impossible?"

12

"Her name is on the register, and my mother knew her well. She was mysterious then, and I think my mother got into her power, but of that I am not certain. Anyhow, Edith and I adore her, don't we, Edie?"

She laid her hand affectionately on her sister's arm. Edith Dallas did not speak, but her face was careworn. After a time she said slowly:

"Madame Sara is uncanny and terrible."

There is, perhaps, no business imaginable--not even a lawyer's--that engenders suspicions more than mine. I hate all mysteries--both in persons and things. Mysteries are my natural enemies; I felt now that this woman was a distinct mystery That she was interested in me I did not doubt, perhaps because she was afraid of me.

The rest of the voyage passed pleasantly enough. The more I saw of Mrs. Selby and her sister the more I liked them. They were quiet, simple, and straightforward. I felt sure that they were both as good as gold.

We parted at Waterloo, Jack and his wife and her sister going to Jack's house in Eaton Square, and I returning to my quarters in St John's Wood. I had a house there, with a long garden, at the bottom of which was my laboratory, the laboratory that was the pride of my life, it being, I fondly considered, the best private laboratory in London. There I spent all my spare time making experiments and trying this chemical combination and the other, living in hopes of doing great things some day, for Werner's Agency was not to be the end of my career. Nevertheless, it interested me thoroughly, and I was not sorry to get back to my commercial conundrums.

The next day, just before I started to go to my place of business, Jack Selby was announced.

"I want you to help me," he said. "I have been already trying in a sort of general way to get information about my brother-in-law, but all in vain. There is no such person in any of the directories. Can you put me on the road to discovery?"

I said I could and would if he would leave the matter in my hands.

"With pleasure," he replied. "You see how we are fixed up. Neither Edith nor Bee can get money with any regularity until the man is found. I cannot imagine why he hides himself."

"I will insert advertisements in the personal columns of the newspapers," I said, "and request anyone who can give information to communicate with me at my office. I will also give instructions to all the branches of my firm, as well as to my head assistants in London, to keep their eyes open for any news. You may be quite certain that in a week or two we shall know all about him."

Selby appeared cheered at this proposal and, having begged of me to call upon his wife and her sister as soon as possible, took his leave.

On that very day advertisements were drawn up and sent to several newspapers and inquiry agents; but week after week passed without the slightest result. Selby got very fidgety at the delay. He was never happy except in my presence, and insisted on my coming, whenever I had time, to his house. I was glad to do so, for I took an interest both in him and his belongings, and as to Madame Sara I could not get her out of my head. One day Mrs. Selby said to me:

"Have you ever been to see Madame? I know she would like to show you her shop and general surroundings."

"I did promise to call upon her," I answered, "but have not had time to do so yet."

"Will you come with me tomorrow morning?" asked Edith Dallas, suddenly.

She turned red as she spoke, and the worried, uneasy expression became more marked on her face. I had noticed for some time that she had been looking both nervous and depressed. I had first observed this peculiarity about her on board the *Norham Castle*, but, as time went on, instead of lessening it grew worse. Her face for so young a woman was haggard; she started at each sound, and Madame Sara's name was never spoken in her presence without her evincing almost undue emotion.

"Will you come with me?" she said, with great eagerness.

I immediately promised, and the next day, about eleven o'clock, Edith Dallas and I found ourselves in a hansom driving to Madame Sara's shop. We reached it in a few minutes, and found an unpretentious little place wedged in between a hosier's on one side and a cheap print-seller's on the other. In the windows of the shop were pyramids of perfume bottles, with scintillating facet stoppers tied with colored ribbons. We stepped out of the hansom and went indoors.

Inside the shop were a couple of steps, which led to a door of solid mahogany.

"This is the entrance to her private house," said Edith, and she pointed to a small brass plate, on which was engraved the name--"Madame Sara, *Parfumeuse*".

Edith touched an electric bell and the door was immediately opened by a smartly-dressed page-boy. He looked at Miss Dallas as if he knew her very well, and said:

"Madame is within, and is expecting you, miss."

He ushered us both into a quiet-looking room, soberly but handsomely furnished. He left us, closing the door. Edith turned to me.

"Do you know where we are?" she asked.

"We are standing at present in a small room just behind Madame Sara's shop," I answered. "Why are you so excited, Miss Dallas? What is the matter with you?"

"We are on the threshold of a magician's cave," she replied. "We shall soon be face to face with the most marvelous woman in the whole of London. There is no one like her."

"And you--fear her?" I said, dropping my voice to a whisper.

She started, stepped back, and with great difficulty recovered her composure. At that moment the page-boy returned to conduct us through a series of small waiting-rooms, and we soon found ourselves in the presence of Madame herself.

"Ah!" she said, with a smile. "This is delightful. You have kept your word, Edith, and I am greatly obliged to you. I will now show Mr. Druce some of the mysteries of my trade.

But understand, sir," she added, "that I shall not tell you any of my real secrets, only as you would like to know something about me you shall."

"How can you tell I should like to know about you?" I asked.

She gave me an earnest glance which somewhat astonished me, and then she said:

"Knowledge is power; don't refuse what I am willing to give. Edith, you will not object to waiting here while I show Mr. Druce through the rooms. First observe this room, Mr. Druce. It is lighted only from the roof. When the door shuts it automatically locks itself, so that any intrusion from without is impossible. This is my sanctum sanctorum--a faint odor of perfume pervades the room. This is a hot day, but the room itself is cool. What do you think of it all?"

"THIS IS MY SANCTUM SANCTORUM."

I made no answer. She walked to the other end and motioned to me to accompany her. There stood a polished oak square table, on which lay an array of extraordinary looking articles and implements - stoppered bottles full of strange medicaments, mirrors, plane and concave, brushes, sprays, sponges, delicate needle-pointed instruments of bright steel, tiny lancets, and forceps. Facing this table was a chair, like those used by dentists. Above the chair hung electric lights in powerful reflectors, and lenses like bull's-eye lanterns. Another chair, supported on a glass pedestal, was kept there, Madame Sara informed me, for administering static electricity. There were dry-cell batteries for the continuous currents and induction coils for Faradic currents. There were also platinum needles for burning out the roots of hairs.

Madame took me from this room into another, where a still more formidable array of instruments was to be found. Here were a wooden operating table and chloroform and ether apparatus. When I had looked at everything, she turned to me.

"Now you know," she said. "I am a doctor - perhaps a quack. These are my secrets. By means of these I live and flourish."

She turned her back on me and walked into the other room with the light, springy step of youth. Edith Dallas white as a ghost, was waiting for us.

"You have done your duty, my child," said Madame. "Mr. Druce has seen just what I want him to see. I am very much obliged to you both. We shall meet tonight at Lady Farringdon's 'At Home'. Until then, farewell."

When we got into the street and were driving back again to Eaton Square, I turned to Edith.

"Many things puzzle me about your friend," I said, "but perhaps none more than this. By what possible means can a woman who owns to being the possessor of a shop obtain the *entrée* to some of the best houses in London? Why does Society open her doors to this woman, Miss Dallas?"

"I cannot quite tell you," was her reply. "I only know the fact that wherever she goes she is welcomed and treated with consideration, and wherever she fails to appear there is a universally expressed feeling of regret."

I had also been invited to Lady Farringdon's reception that evening, and I went there in a state of great curiosity. There was no doubt that Madame interested me. I was not sure of her. Beyond doubt there was a mystery attached to her, and also, for some unaccountable reason, she wished both to propitiate and defy me. Why was this?

I arrived early, and was standing in the crush near the head of the staircase when Madame was announced. She wore the richest white satin and quantities of diamonds. I saw her hostess bend towards her and talk eagerly. I noticed Madame's reply and the pleased expression that crossed Lady Farringdon's face. A few minutes later a man with a foreign-looking face and long beard sat down before the grand piano. He played a light prelude and Madame Sara began to sing. Her voice was sweet and low, with an extraordinary pathos in it. It was the sort of voice that penetrates to the heart. There was an instant pause in the gay chatter. She sang amidst perfect silence, and when the song had come to an end there followed a *furor* of applause. I was just turning to say something to my nearest neighbor when I observed Edith Dallas, who was standing close by. Her eyes met mine; she laid her hand on my sleeve.

"The room is hot," she said, half panting as she spoke. "Take me out on the balcony."

I did so. The atmosphere of the reception-rooms was almost intolerable, but it was comparatively cool in the open air.

"I must not lose sight of her," she said, suddenly.

"Of whom?" I asked, somewhat astonished at her words.

"Of Sara."

"She is there," I said. "You can see her from where you stand."

We happened to be alone. I came a little closer.

"Why are you afraid of her?" I asked.

"Are you sure that we shall not be heard?" was her answer.

"She terrifies me," were her next words.

"I will not betray your confidence, Miss Dallas. Will you not trust me? You ought to give me a reason for your fears."

"I cannot--I dare not; I have said far too much already. Don't keep me, Mr. Druce. She must not find us together."

As she spoke she pushed her way through the crowd, and before I could stop her was standing by Madame Sara's side.

The reception in Portland Place was, I remember, on the 26th of July. Two days later the Selbys were to give their final "At Home" before leaving for the country. I was, of course, invited to be present, and Madame was also there. She had never been dressed more splendidly, nor had she ever before looked younger or more beautiful. Wherever she went all eyes followed her. As a rule her dress was simple, almost like what a girl would wear, but tonight she chose rich Oriental stuffs made of many colors, and absolutely glittering with gems. Her golden hair was studded with diamonds. Round her neck she wore turquoise and diamonds mixed. There were many younger women in the room, but not the youngest nor the fairest had a chance beside Madame. It was not mere beauty of appearance, it was charm--charm which carries all before it.

I saw Miss Dallas, looking slim and tall and pale, standing at a little distance. I made my way to her side. Before I had time to speak she bent towards me.

"Is she not divine?" she whispered. "She bewilders and delights everyone. She is taking London by storm."

"Then you are not afraid of her tonight?" I said.

"I fear her more than ever. She has cast a spell over me. But listen, she is going to sing again."

I had not forgotten the song that Madame had given us at the Farringdons', and stood still to listen. There was a complete hush in the room. Her voice floated over the heads of the assembled guests in a dreamy Spanish song. Edith told me that it was a slumber song, and that Madame boasted of her power of putting almost anyone to sleep who listened to her rendering of it.

"She has many patients who suffer from insomnia," whispered the girl, "and she generally cures them with that song, and that alone. Ah! We must not talk; she will hear us."

Before I could reply Selby came hurrying up. He had not noticed Edith. He caught me by the arm.

"Come just for a minute into this window, Dixon," he said. "I must speak to you. I suppose you have no news with regard my brother-in-law?"

"Not a word," I answered.

"To tell you the truth, I am getting terribly put out over the matter. We cannot settle any of our money affairs just because this man chooses to lose himself. My wife's lawyers wired to Brazil yesterday, but even his bankers do not know anything about him."

"The whole thing is a question of time," was my answer. "When are you off to Hampshire?"

"On Saturday."

As Selby said the last words he looked around him, then he dropped his voice.

"I want to say something else. The more I see - " he nodded towards Madame Sara--"the less I like her. Edith is getting into a very strange state. Have you not noticed it? And the worst of it is my wife is also infected. I suppose it is that dodge of the woman's for patching people up and making them beautiful. Doubtless the temptation is over-powering in the case of a plain woman, but Beatrice is beautiful herself and young. What can she have to do with cosmetics and complexion pills?"

"You don't mean to tell me that your wife has consulted Madame Sara as a doctor?"

"Not exactly, but she has gone to her about her teeth. She complained of toothache lately, and Madame's dentistry is renowned. Edith is constantly going to her for one thing or another, but then Edith is infatuated."

As Jack said the last words he went over to speak to someone else, and before I could leave the seclusion of the window I perceived Edith Dallas and Madame Sara in earnest conversation together. I could not help overhearing the following words:

"Don't come to me tomorrow. Get into the country as soon as you can. It is far and away the best thing to do."

As Madame spoke she turned swiftly and caught my eyes. She bowed, and the peculiar look, the sort of challenge, she had given me before flashed over her face. It made me uncomfortable, and during the night that followed I could not get it out of my head. I remembered what Selby had said with regard to his wife and her money affairs. Beyond doubt he had married into a mystery--a mystery that Madame knew all about. There was a very big money interest, and strange things happen when millions are concerned.

The next morning I had just risen and was sitting at breakfast when a note was handed to me. It came by special messenger, and was marked "Urgent". I tore it open. These were its contents:--

"My Dear Druce, A terrible blow has fallen on us. My sister-in-law, Edith, was taken suddenly ill this morning at breakfast. The nearest doctor was sent for, but he could do nothing, as she died half an hour ago. Do come and see me and if you know any very clever specialist bring him with you. My wife is utterly stunned by the shock.--Yours, Jack Selby

I read the note twice before I could realize what it meant. Then I rushed out and, hailing the first hansom I met, said the man:

"Drive to No. 192, Victoria Street, as quickly as you can."

Here lived a certain Mr. Eric Vandeleur, an old friend of mine and the police surgeon for the Westminster district, which included Eaton Square. No shrewder or sharper fellow existed than Vandeleur, and the present case was essentially in his province, both legally and professionally. He was not at his flat when I arrived, having already gone down to the court. Here I accordingly hurried, and was informed that he was in the mortuary.

For a man who, as it seemed to me, lived in a perpetual atmosphere of crime and violence, of death and coroners' courts, his habitual cheerfulness and brightness of manner were remarkable. Perhaps it was only the reaction from his work, for he had the reputation of being one of the most astute experts of the day in medical jurisprudence, and the most skilled analyst in toxicological cases on the Metropolitan Police staff. Before I could send him word that I wanted to see him I heard a door bang, and Vandeleur came hurrying down the passage, putting on his coat as he rushed along.

"Halloa!" he cried. "I haven't seen you for ages. Do you want me?"

"Yes, very urgently," I answered. "Are you busy?"

"Head over ears, my dear chap. I cannot give you a moment now, but perhaps later on."

24

"What is it? You look excited."

"I have got to go to Eaton Square like the wind, but come along, if you like, and tell me on the way."

"Capital," I cried. "The thing has been reported then? You are going to Mr. Selby's, No. 34a; then I am going with you."

He looked at me in amazement.

"But the case has only just been reported. What can you possibly know about it?"

"Everything. Let us take this hansom, and I will tell you as we go along."

As we drove to Eaton Square I quickly explained the situation, glancing now and then at Vandeleur's bright, clean-shaven face. He was no longer Eric Vandeleur, the man with the latest club story and the merry twinkle in his blue eyes: he was Vandeleur the medical jurist, with a face like a mask, his lower jaw slightly protruding and features very fixed.

"The thing promises to be serious," he replied, as I finished, "but I can do nothing until after the autopsy. Here we are and there is my man waiting for me; he has been smart."

On the steps stood an official-looking man in uniform who saluted.

"Coroner's officer," explained Vandeleur.

We entered the silent, darkened house. Selby was standing in the hall. He came to meet us. I introduced him to Vandeleur, and he at once led us into the dining-room, where we found Dr. Osborne, whom Selby had called in when the alarm of Edith's illness had been first given. Dr. Osborne was a pale, under-sized, very young man. His face expressed considerable alarm. Vandeleur, however, managed to put him completely at his ease.

"I will have a chat with you in a few minutes, Dr. Osborne," he said; "but first I must get Mr. Selby's report. Will you please tell me, sir, exactly what occurred?"

"Certainly," he answered. "We had a reception here last night, and my sister-in-law did not go to bed until early morning; she was in bad spirits, but otherwise in her usual health. My wife went into her room after she was in bed, and told me later on that she had found Edith in hysterics, and could not get her to explain anything. We both talked about taking her to the country without delay. Indeed, our intention was to get off this afternoon."

"Well?" said Vandeleur.

We had breakfast about half-past nine, and Miss Dallas came down, looking quite in her usual health, and in apparently good spirits. She ate with appetite, and, as it happened, she and my wife were both helped from the same dish. The meal had nearly come to end when she jumped up from the table, uttered a sharp cry, turned very pale, pressed her hand to her side, and ran out of the room. My wife immediately followed her. She came back again in a minute or two, and said that Edith was in violent pain, and begged of me to send for a doctor. Dr. Osborne lives just round the corner. He came at once, but she died almost immediately after his arrival."

"SHE JUMPED UP FROM THE TABLE AND UTTERED A SHARP CRY."

"You were in the room?" asked Vandeleur, turning to Osborne.

"Yes," he replied. "She was conscious to the last moment, and died suddenly."

"Did she tell you anything?"

"No, except to assure me that she had not eaten any food that day until she had come down to breakfast. After the death occurred I sent immediately to report the case, locked the door of the room where the poor girl's body is, and saw also that nobody touched anything on this table."

Vandeleur rang the bell and a servant appeared. He gave quick orders. The entire remains of the meal were collected and taken charge of, and then he and the coroner's officer went upstairs.

When we were alone Selby sank into a chair. His face was quite drawn and haggard.

"It is the horrible suddenness of the thing which is so appalling," he cried. "As to Beatrice, I don't believe she will ever be the same again. She was deeply attached to Edith. Edith was nearly ten years her senior, and always acted the part of mother to her. This is a sad beginning to our life. I can scarcely think collectedly."

I remained with him a little longer, and then, as Vandeleur did not return, went back to my own house. There I could settle to nothing, and when Vandeleur rang me up on the telephone about six o'clock I hurried off to his rooms. As soon as I arrived I saw that Selby was with him, and the expression on both their faces told me the truth.

"This is a bad business," said Vandeleur. "Miss Dallas has died from swallowing poison. An exhaustive analysis and examination have been made, and a powerful poison, unknown to European toxicologists, has been found. This is strange enough, but how it has been administered is a puzzle. I confess, at the present moment, we are all non-plussed. It certainly was not in the remains of the breakfast, and we have her dying evidence that she took nothing else. Now, a poison with such appalling potency would take effect quickly. It is evident that she was quite well when she came to breakfast, and that the poison began to work towards the close of the meal. But how did she get it? This question, however, I shall deal with later on. The more immediate point is this. The situation is a serious one in view of the monetary issues and the value of the lady's life. From the aspects of the case, her undoubted sanity and her affection for her sister, we may almost exclude the idea of suicide. We must, therefore, call it murder. This harmless, innocent lady is struck down by the hand of an assassin, and with such devilish cunning that no trace or clue is left behind. For such an act there must have been some very powerful motive, and the person who designed and executed it must be a criminal the highest order of scientific ability. Mr. Selby has been telling me the exact financial position of the poor lady, and also of his own young wife. The absolute disappearance of the step-brother, in view of his previous character, is in the highest degree strange. Knowing, as we do, that between him and two million sterling there stood two lives--*one is taken!*"

A deadly sensation of cold seized me as Vandeleur uttered these last words. I glanced at Selby. His face was colorless and the pupils of his eyes were contracted, as though he saw something which terrified him.

"What happened once may happen again," continued Vandeleur. "We are in the presence of a great mystery, and I counsel you, Mr. Selby, to guard your wife with the utmost care."

These words, falling from a man of Vandeleur's position and authority on such matters, were sufficiently shocking for me to hear, but for Selby to be given such a solemn warning about his young and beautiful and newly-married wife, who was all the world to him, was terrible indeed. He leant his head on his hands.

"Mercy on us!" he muttered. "Is this a civilized country when death can walk abroad like this, invisible, not to be avoided? Tell me, Mr. Vandeleur, what I must do."

"You must be guided by me," said Vandeleur, "and, believe me, there is no witchcraft in the world. I shall place a detective in your household immediately. Don't be alarmed; he will come to you in plain clothes and will simply act as a servant. Nevertheless, nothing can be done to your wife without his knowledge. As to you, Druce," he continued, turning to me, "the police are doing all they can to find this man Silva, and I ask you to help them with your big agency, and to begin at once. Leave your friend to me. Wire instantly if you hear news."

"You may rely on me," I said, and a moment later I had left the room.

As I walked rapidly down the street the thought of Madame Sara, her shop and its mysterious background, its surgical instruments, its operating-table, its induction coils, came back to me. And yet what could Madame Sara have to do with the present strange, inexplicable mystery?

The thought had scarcely crossed my mind before I heard a clatter alongside the curb, and turning round I saw a smart open carriage, drawn by a pair of horses, standing there. I also heard my own name. I turned. Bending out of the carriage was Madame Sara.

"I saw you going by, Mr. Druce. I have only just heard the news about poor Edith Dallas. I am terribly shocked and upset. I have been to the house, but they would not admit me. Have you heard what was the cause of her death?"

Madame"s blue eyes filled with tears as she spoke.

"I am not at liberty to disclose what I have heard Madame," I answered, "since I am officially connected with the affair."

Her eyes narrowed. The brimming tears dried as though by magic. Her glance became scornful.

"Thank you," she answered; "your reply tells me that she did not die naturally. How very appalling! But I must not keep you. Can I drive you anywhere?"

"No, thank you."

"Good-bye, then."

She made a sign to the coachman, and as the carriage rolled away turned to look back at me. her face wore the defiant expression I had seen there more than once. Could she be connected with the affair? The thought came upon me with a violence that seemed almost conviction. Yet I had no reason for it--none.

To find Henry Joachim Silva was now my principal thought. Advertisements were widely circulated. My staff had instructions to make every possible inquiry, with large money rewards as incitements. The collateral branches of other agencies throughout Brazil were communicated with by cable, and all the Scotland Yard channels were used. Still there was no result. The newspapers took up the case; there were paragraphs in most of them with regard to the missing step-brother and the mysterious death of Edith Dallas. Then someone got hold of the story of the will, and this was retailed with many additions for the benefit of the public. At the inquest the jury returned the following verdict:--

"We find that Miss Edith Dallas died from taking poison of unknown name, but by whom or how administered there is no evidence to say."

This unsatisfactory state of things was destined to change quite suddenly. On the 6th of August, as I was seated in my office, a note was brought me by a private messenger. It ran as follows:--

"Norfolk Hotel, Strand.

"Dear Sir,--

I have just arrived in London from Brazil, and have seen your advertisements. I was about to insert one myself n order to find the whereabouts of my sisters. I am a great invalid and unable to leave my room. Can you come to see me at he earliest possible moment? —

Yours

"Henry Joachim Silva."

In uncontrollable excitement I hastily dispatched two telegrams, one to Selby and the other to Vandeleur, begging of them to be with me, without fail, as soon as possible. So the man had never been in England at all. The situation was more bewildering than ever. One thing, at least was probably-- Edith Dallas's death was not due to her step-brother. Soon after half-past six Selby arrived, and Vandeleur walked in ten minutes later. I told them what had occurred and showed them the letter. In half an hour's time we reached the hotel, and on stating who I was we were shown into a room on f the first floor by Silva's private servant. Resting in an arm-chair, as were entered, sat a man; his face was terribly thin. The eyes and cheeks were so sunken that the face had almost the appearance of a skull. He made no effort to rise when we entered, and glanced from one of us to the other with the utmost astonishment. I at once introduced myself and explained who we ere. He then waved his hand for his man to retire.

"You have not heard the news, of course, Mr. Silva?" I said.

"News! What?" He glanced up to me and seemed to read something in my face. he started back in his chair.

"Good heavens!" he replied. "Do you allude to my sisters? Tell me, quickly, are they alive?"

"Your elder sister died on the 29th of July, and there is every reason to believe her death was caused by foul play."

As I uttered these words the change that passed over his face was fearful to witness. He did not speak, but remained motionless. His claw-like hands clutched the arms of the chair, his eyes were fixed and staring, as though they would start from their hollow sockets, the color of his skin was like clay. I heard Selby breathe quickly behind me, and Vandeleur stepped towards the man and laid his hand on his shoulder.

"Tell us what you know of this matter," he said sharply.

Recovering himself with an effort, the invalid began in a tremulous voice:

"Listen closely, for you must act quickly. I am indirectly responsible for this fearful thing. My life has been a wild and wasted one, and now I am dying. The doctors tell me I cannot live a month, for I have a large aneurism of the heart. Eighteen months ago I was in Rio. I was living fast and gambled heavily. Among my fellow-gamblers was a man much older than myself. His name was José Aranjo. He was, if anything, a greater gambler than I. One night we played alone. The stakes ran high until they reached a big figure. By daylight I had lost to him nearly £200,000. Though I am a rich man in point of income under my uncle's will, I could not pay a twentieth part of that sum. This man knew my financial position, and, in addition to a sum of £5,000 paid down, I gave him a document. I must have been mad to do so. The document was this--it was duly witnessed and attested by a lawyer--that, in the event of my surviving my two sisters and thus inheriting the whole of my uncle's vast wealth, half a million should go to José Aranjo. I felt I was breaking up at the time, and the chances of my inheriting the money were small. Immediately after the completion of the document this man left Rio, and I then heard a great deal about him that I had not previously known. He was a man of the queerest antecedents, partly Indian, partly Italian. He had spent many years of his life amongst the Indians. I heard also that he was as cruel as he was clever, and possessed some wonderful secrets of poisoning unknown to the West. I thought a great deal about this, for I knew that by signing that document I had placed the lives of my two sisters between him and a fortune. I came to Para six weeks ago, only to learn that one of my sisters was married and that both had gone to England. Ill as I was, I determined to follow them in order to warn them. I also wanted to arrange matters with you, Mr. Selby."

"I HAD LOST TO HIM NEARLY £200,000!"

"One moment, sir," I broke in, suddenly. "Do you happen to be aware if this man, José Aranjo, knew a woman calling herself Madame Sara?"

"Knew her?" cried Silva. "Very well indeed, and so, for that matter, did I. Aranjo and Madame Sara were the best friends, and constantly met. She called herself a professional beautifier--was very handsome, and had secrets for the pursuing of her trade unknown even to Aranjo."

"Good heavens!" I cried, "and the woman is now in London. She returned here with Mrs. Selby and Miss Dallas. Edith was very much influenced by her, and was constantly with her. There is no doubt in my mind that she is guilty. I have suspected her for some time, but I could not find a motive. Now the motive appears. You surely can have her arrested?"

Vandeleur made no reply. He gave me a strange look, then he turned to Selby.

"Has your wife also consulted Madame Sara?" he asked, sharply.

"Yes, she went to her once about her teeth but has not been to the shop since Edith's death. I begged of her not to see the woman, and she promised me faithfully she would not do so."

"Has she any medicines or lotions given to her by Madame Sara--does she follow any line of treatment advised by her?"

"No, I am certain on that point."

"Very well. I will see your wife tonight in order to ask her some questions. You must both leave town at once. Go to your country house and settle there. I am quite serious when I say that Mrs. Selby is in the utmost possible danger until after the death of her brother. We must leave you now, Mr. Silva. All business affairs must wait for the present. It is absolutely necessary that Mrs. Selby should leave London at once. Good night, sir. I shall give myself the pleasure of calling on you tomorrow morning."

35

We took leave of the sick man. As soon as we got into the street Vandeleur stopped.

"I must leave it to you, Selby," he said, "to judge how much of this matter you tell to your wife. Were I you I would explain everything. The time for immediate action has arrived, and she is a brave and sensible woman. From this moment you must watch all the foods and liquids that she takes. She must never be out of your sight or out of the sight of some other trustworthy companion."

"I shall, of course, watch my wife myself," said Selby. "But the thing is enough to drive one mad."

"I will go with you to the country, Selby," I said, suddenly.

"Ah!" cried Vandeleur, "that is the best thing possible, and what I wanted to propose. Go, all of you, by an early train tomorrow."

"Then I will be off home at once to make arrangements," I said. "I will meet you, Selby, at Waterloo for the first train to Cronsmoor tomorrow."

As I was turning away Vandeleur caught my arm.

"I am glad you are going with them," he said. "I shall write to you tonight re instructions. Never be without a loaded revolver. Goodnight."

By 6.15 the next morning Selby, his wife, and I were in a reserved, locked, first-class compartment, speeding rapidly west. The servants and Mrs. Selby's own special maid were in a separate carriage. Selby's face showed signs of a sleepless night, and presented a striking contrast to the fair, fresh face of the girl round whom this strange battle raged. Her husband

36

had told her everything, and though still suffering terribly from the shock and grief of her sister's death, her face was calm and full of repose.

A carriage was waiting for us at Cronsmoor, and by half-nine we arrived at the old home of the Selbys, nestling amid its oaks and elms. Everything was done to make the homecoming of the bride as cheerful as circumstances would permit, but a gloom, impossible to lift, overshadowed Selby himself. He could scarcely rouse himself to take the slightest interest in anything.

The following morning I received a letter from Vandeleur. It was very short, and once more impressed on me the necessity of caution. He said that two eminent physicians had examined Silva, and the verdict was that he could not live a month. Until his death precautions must be strictly observed.

The day was cloudless, and after breakfast I was just starting out for a stroll when the butler brought me a telegram. I tore it open; it was from Vandeleur.

"Prohibit all food until I arrive. Am coming down," were the words. I hurried into the study and gave it to Selby. He it and looked up at me.

"Find out the first train and go and meet him, old chap," he said. "Let us hope that this means an end of the hideous affair."

I went into the hall and looked up the trains. The next arrived at Cronsmoor at 10.45. I then strolled round to the stables and ordered a carriage, after which I walked up and down on the drive. There was no doubt that something strange had happened. Vandeleur coming down so suddenly must mean a final clearing up of the mystery. I had just turned round at the lodge gates to wait for the carriage when the sound of wheels and of horses galloping struck on my ears. The gates were swung open, and Vandeleur in an open fly dashed through them. Before I could recover from my surprise he was out of the vehicle and at my side. He carried a small black bag in his hand.

"I came down by special train," he said, speaking quickly. "There is not a moment to lose. Come at once. Is Mrs. Selby all right?"

"What do you mean?" I replied. "Of course she is. Do you suppose that she is in danger?"

"Deadly," was his answer. "Come."

We dashed up to the house together. Selby, who had heard our steps, came to meet us.

"Mr. Vandeleur," he cried. "What is it? How did you come?"

"By special train, Mr. Selby. And I want to see your wife at once. It will be necessary to perform a very trifling operation."

"Operation!" he exclaimed.

"Yes; at once."

We made our way through the hall and into the morning-room, where Mrs. Selby was busily engaged reading and answering letters. She started up when she saw Vandeleur and uttered an exclamation of surprise.

"What has happened?" she asked.

Vandeleur went up to her and took her hand.

"Do not be alarmed," he said, "for I have come to put all your fears to rest. Now, please, listen to me. When you visited Madame Sara with your sister, did you go for medical advice?"

The color rushed into her face.

"One of my teeth ached," she answered. "I went to her about that. She is, as I suppose you know, a most wonderful dentist. She examined the tooth, found that it required stopping, and got an assistant, a Brazilian, I think, to do it."

"And your tooth has been comfortable ever since?"

"Yes, quite. She had one of Edith's stopped at the same time."

"Will you kindly sit down and show me which was the tooth into which the stopping was put?"

She did so.

"This was the one," she said, pointing with her finger to one in the lower jaw. "What do you mean? Is there anything wrong?"

Vandeleur examined the tooth long and carefully. There was a sudden rapid movement of his hand, and a sharp cry from Mrs. Selby. With the deftness of long practice, and a powerful wrist, he had extracted the tooth with one wrench. The suddenness of the whole thing, startling as it was, was not so strange as his next movement.

"Send Mrs. Selby's maid to her," he said, turning to her husband; "then come, both of you, into the next room."

The maid was summoned. Poor Mrs. Selby had sunk back in her chair, terrified and half fainting. A moment later Selby joined us in the dining-room.

"That's right," said Vandeleur; "close the door, will you?" He opened his black bag and brought out several instruments. With one he removed the stopping from the tooth. It was quite soft and came away easily. Then from the bag he produced a small guinea-pig, which he requested me to hold. He pressed the sharp instrument into the tooth, and opening the mouth of the little animal placed the point on the tongue. The effect was instantaneous. The little head fell on to one of my hands--the guinea-pig was dead. Vandeleur was white as a sheet. He hurried up to Selby and wrung his hand.

"Thank heaven!" he said, "I've been in time, but only just. Your wife is safe. This stopping would hardly have held another hour. I have been thinking all night over the mystery of your sister-in-law's death, and over every minute detail of evidence as to how the poison could have been administered. Suddenly the coincidence of both sisters having had their teeth stopped struck me as remarkable. Like a flash the solution came to me. The more I considered it the more I felt that I was right; but by what fiendish cunning such a scheme could have been conceived and executed is beyond my power to explain. The poison is very like hyoscine, one of the worst toxic-alkaloids known, so violent in its deadly proportions that the amount that would go into a tooth would cause almost instant death. It has been kept in by a gutta-percha stopping, certain to come out within a month, probably earlier, and most probably during mastication of food. The person would die either immediately or after a very few minutes, and no one would connect a visit to the dentist with a death a month afterwards."

What followed can be told in a very few words. Madame Sara was arrested on suspicion. She appeared before the magistrate, looking innocent and beautiful, and managed during her evidence completely to baffle that acute individual. She denied nothing, but declared that the poison must have been put into the tooth by one of the two Brazilians whom she had lately engaged to help her with her dentistry. She had her suspicions with regard to these men soon afterwards, and had dismissed them. She believed that they were in the pay of José Aranjo, but she could not tell anything for certain. Thus Madame escaped conviction. I was certain that she was guilty, but there was not a shadow of real proof. A month later Silva died, and Selby is now a double millionaire.

II. *The Blood Red Cross.*

IN the month of November in the year 1899 I found myself a guest in the house of one of my oldest friends-- George Rowland. His beautiful place in Yorkshire was an ideal holiday resort. It went by the name of Rowland's Folly, and had been built on the site of a former dwelling in the reign of the first George. The house was now replete with every modern luxury. It, however, very nearly cost its first owner, if not the whole of his fortune, yet the most precious heirloom of the family. This was a pearl necklace of almost fabulous value. It had been secured as booty by a certain Geoffrey Rowland at the time of the Battle of Agincourt, had originally been the property of one of the Dukes of Genoa, and had even for a short time been in the keeping of the Pope. From the moment that Geoffrey Rowland took possession of the necklace there had been several attempts made to deprive him of it. Sword, fire, water, poison, had all been used, but ineffectually. The necklace with its eighty pearls, smooth, symmetrical, pear-shaped, of a translucent white color and with a subdued iridescent sheen, was still in the possession of the family, and was likely to remain there, as George Rowland told me, until the end of time. Each bride wore the necklace on her wedding-day, after which it was put into the strong-room and, as a rule, never seen again until the next bridal occasion. The pearls were roughly estimated as worth from two to three thousand pounds each, but the historical value of the necklace put the price almost beyond the dreams of avarice.

It was reported that in the autumn of that same year an American millionaire had offered to buy it from the family at their own price, but as no terms would be listened to the negotiations fell through.

George Rowland belonged to the oldest and proudest family in the West Riding, and no man looked a better gentleman or more fit to uphold ancient dignities than he. He was proud to boast that from the earliest days no stain of dishonor had touched his house, that the women of the family were as good as the men, their blood pure, their morals irreproachable, their ideas lofty.

I went to Rowland's Folly in November, and found a pleasant, hospitable, and cheerful hostess in Lady Kennedy, Rowland's only sister. Antonia Ripley was, however, the centre of all interest. Rowland was engaged to Antonia, and the history was romantic. Lady Kennedy told me all about it.

"She is a penniless girl without family," remarked the good woman, somewhat snappishly. "I can't imagine what George was thinking of."

"How did your brother meet her?" I asked.

"We were both in Italy last autumn; we were staying in Naples, at the Vesuve. An English lady was staying there of the name of Studley. She died while we were at the hotel. She had under her charge a young girl, the same Antonia who is now engaged to my brother. Before her death she begged of us to befriend her, saying that the child was without money and without friends. All Mrs. Studley's money died with her. We promised, not being able to do otherwise. George fell in love almost at first sight. Little Antonia was provided for by becoming engaged to my brother. I have nothing to say against the girl, but I dislike this sort of match very much. Besides, she is more foreign than English."

"Cannot Miss Ripley tell you anything about her history?"

"Nothing, except that Mrs. Studley adopted her when she was a tiny child. She says, also, that she has a dim recollection of a large building crowded with people, and a man who stretched out his arms to her and was taken forcibly away. That is all. She is quite a nice child, and amiable, with touching ways and a pathetic face; but no one knows what her ancestry was. Ah, there you are, Antonia! What is the matter now?"

The girl tripped across the room. She was like a young fawn; of a smooth, olive complexion--dark of eye and mysteriously beautiful, with the graceful step which is seldom granted to an English girl.

"My lace dress has come," she said. "Markham is unpacking it--but the bodice is made with a low neck."

Lady Kennedy frowned.

"You are too absurd, Antonia," she said. "Why won't you dress like other girls? I assure you that peculiarity of yours of always wearing your dress high in the evening annoys George."

44

"Does it?" she answered, and she stepped back and put her hand to her neck just below the throat---a constant habit of hers, as I afterwards had occasion to observe.

"It disturbs him very much," said Lady Kennedy. "He spoke to me about it only yesterday. Please understand, Antonia, that at the ball you cannot possibly wear a dress high to your throat. It cannot be permitted."

"I shall be properly dressed on the night of the ball," replied the girl.

Her face grew crimson, then deadly pale.

"It only wants a fortnight to that time, but I shall be ready."

There was a solemnity about her words. She turned and left the room.

"Antonia is a very trying character," said Lady Kennedy. "Why won't she act like other girls? She makes such a fuss about wearing a proper evening dress that she tries my patience--but she is all crotchets."

"A sweet little girl for all that," was my answer.

"Yes; men like her."

Soon afterwards, as I was strolling, on the terrace, I met Miss Ripley. She was sitting in a low chair. I noticed how small, and slim, and young she looked, and how pathetic was the expression of her little face. When she saw me she seemed to hesitate; then she came to my side.

"May I walk with you, Mr. Druce?" she asked.

"I am quite at your service," I answered. "Where shall we go?"

"It doesn't matter. I want to know if you will help me."

"Certainly, if I can, Miss Ripley."

"It is most important. I want to go to London."

"Surely that is not very difficult?"

"They won't allow me to go alone, and they are both very busy. I have just sent a telegram to a friend. I want to see her. I know she will receive me. I want to go to-morrow. May I venture to ask that you should be my escort?"

"My dear Miss Ripley, certainly," I said. "I will help you with pleasure."

"It must be done," she said, in a low voice. "I have put it off too long. When I marry him he shall not be disappointed."

"I do not understand you," I said, "but I will go with you with the greatest willingness."

She smiled; and the next day, much to my own amazement, I found myself traveling first-class up to London, with little Miss Ripley as my companion. Neither Rowland nor his sister had approved; but Antonia had her own way, and the fact that I would escort her cleared off some difficulties. During our journey she bent towards me and said, in a low tone:--

"Have you ever heard of that most wonderful, that great woman, Madame Sara?'

I looked at her intently.

"I have certainly heard of Madame Sara," I said, with emphasis, "but I sincerely trust that you have nothing to do with her."

"I have known her almost all my life," said the girl. "Mrs. Studley knew her also. I love her very much. I trust her. I am going to see her now."

"What do you mean?"

"It was to her I wired yesterday. She will receive me; she will help me. I am returning to the Folly to-night. Will you add to your kindness by escorting me home?"

"Certainly."

At Euston I put my charge into a hansom, arranging to meet her on the departure platform at twenty minutes to six that evening and then taking another hansom drove as fast as I could to Vandeleur's address. During the latter part of my journey to town a sudden, almost unaccountable, desire to consult Vandeleur had taken possession of me. I was lucky enough to find this busiest of men at home and at leisure. He gave an exclamation of delight when my name was announced, and then came towards me with outstretched hand.

"I was just about to wire to you, Druce," he said. "From where have you sprung?"

"From no less a place than Rowland's Folly," was my answer.

"More and more amazing. Then you have met Miss Ripley, George Rowland's *fiancée*?"

"You have heard of the engagement, Vandeleur?"

47

"Who has not? What sort is the young lady?"

"I can tell you all you want to know, for I have traveled up to town with her."

"Ah!"

He was silent for a minute, evidently thinking hard; then drawing a chair near mine he seated himself.

"How long have you been at Rowland's Folly?" he asked.

"Nearly a week. I am to remain until after the wedding. I consider Rowland a lucky man. He is marrying a sweet little girl."

"You think so? By the way, have you ever noticed any peculiarity about her?"

"Only that she is singularly amiable and attractive."

"But any habit--pray think carefully before you answer me."

"Really, Vandeleur, your questions surprise me. Little Miss Ripley is a person with ideas and is not ashamed to stick to her principles. You know, of course, that in a house like Rowland's Folly it is the custom for the ladies to come to dinner in full dress. Now, Miss Ripley won't accommodate herself to this fashion, but *will* wear her dress high to the throat, however gay and festive the occasion."

"Ah! There doesn't seem to be much that, does there?"

"I don't quite agree with you. Pressure has been brought to bear on the girl to make her conform to the usual regulations, and Lady Kennedy, a woman old enough to be her mother, is quite disagreeable on the point."

"But the girl sticks to her determination?"

"Absolutely, although she promises to yield and to wear the conventional dress at the ball given in her honor a week before the wedding."

Vandeleur was silent for nearly a minute; then dropping his voice he said, slowly:--

"Did Miss Ripley ever mention in your presence the name of our mutual foe--Madame Sara?"

"How strange that you should ask! On our journey to town to-day she told me that she knew the woman--she has known her for the greater part of her life--poor child, she even loves her. Vandeleur, that young girl is with Madame Sara now."

"Don't be alarmed, Druce; there is no immediate danger; but I may as well tell you that through my secret agents I have made discoveries which show that Madame has another iron in the fire, that once again she is preparing to convulse Society, and that little Miss Ripley is the victim."

"You must be mistaken."

"So sure am I, that I want your help. You are returning to Rowland's Folly?"

"To-night."

"And Miss Ripley?"

"She goes with me. We meet at Euston for the six o'clock train."

"So far, good. By the way, has Rowland spoken to you lately about the pearl necklace?"

"No; why do you ask?"

"Because I understand that it was his intention to have the pearls slightly altered and reset in order to fit Miss Ripley's slender throat; also to have a diamond clasp affixed in place of the somewhat insecure one at present attached to the string of pearls. Messrs. Theodore and Mark, of Bond Street, were to undertake the commission. All was in preparation, and a messenger, accompanied by two detectives, was to go to Rowland's Folly to fetch the treasure, when the whole thing was countermanded, Rowland having changed his mind and having decided that the strong-room at the Folly was the best place in which to keep the necklace."

"He has not mentioned the subject to me," I said. "How do you know?"

"I have my emissaries. One thing is certain--little Miss Ripley is to wear the pearls on her wedding-day--and the Italian family, distant relatives of the present Duke of Genoa, to whom the pearls belonged, and from whom they were stolen shortly before the Battle of Agincourt, are again taking active steps to secure them. You have heard the story of the American millionaire? Well, that was a blind--the necklace was in reality to be delivered into the hands of the old family as soon as he had purchased it. Now, Druce, this is the state of things: Madame Sara is an adventuress, and the cleverest woman in the world--Miss Ripley is very young and ignorant. Miss Ripley is to wear the pearls on her wedding-day--and Madame wants them. You can infer the rest."

"What do you want me to do?" I asked.

"Go back and watch. If you see anything, to arouse suspicion, wire to me."

"What about telling Rowland?"

"I would rather not consult him. I want to protect Miss Ripley, and at the same time to get Madame into my power. She managed to elude us last time, but she shall not this. My idea is to inveigle her to her ruin. Why, Druce, the woman is being more trusted and run after and admired day by day. She appeals to the greatest foibles of the world. She knows some valuable secrets, and is an adept in the art of restoring beauty and to a certain extent conquering the ravages of time. She is at present aided by an Arab, one of the most dangerous men I have ever seen, with the subtlety of a serpent, and legerdemain in every one of his ten fingers. It is not an easy thing to entrap her."

"And yet you mean to do it?"

"Some day---some day. Perhaps now."

His eyes were bright. I had seldom seen him look more excited.

After a short time I left him. Miss Ripley met me at Euston. She was silent and unresponsive and looked depressed. Once I saw her put her hand to her neck.

"Are you in pain?" I asked.

"You might be a doctor, Mr. Druce, from your question."

"But answer me," I said.

She was silent for a minute; then she said, slowly:--

51

"You are good, and I think I ought to tell you. But will you regard it as a secret? You wonder, perhaps, how it is that I don't wear a low dress in the evening. I will tell you why. On my neck, just below the throat, there grew a wart or mole-- large, brown, and ugly. The Italian doctors would not remove it on account of the position. It lies just over what they said was an *aberrant* artery, and the removal might cause very dangerous hemorrhage. One day Madame saw it; she said the doctors were wrong and that she could easily take it away and leave no mark behind. I hesitated for a long time, but yesterday, when Lady Kennedy spoke to me as she did, I made up my mind. I wired to Madame and went to her to-day. She gave me chloroform and removed the mole. My neck is bandaged up and it smarts a little. I am not to remove the bandage until she sees me again. She is very pleased with the result, and says that my neck will now be beautiful like other women's, and that I can on the night of the ball wear the lovely Brussels lace dress that Lady Kennedy has given me. That is my secret. Will you respect it?"

I promised, and soon afterwards we reached the end of our journey.

A few days went by. One morning at breakfast I noticed that the little signora only played with her food. An open letter lay by her plate. Rowland, by whose side she always sat, turned to her.

"What is the matter, Antonia?" he said. "Have you had an unpleasant letter?"

"It is from----"

"From whom, dear?"

"Madame Sara."

"What did I hear you say?" cried Lady Kennedy.

52

"I have had a letter from Madame Sara, Lady Kennedy."

"That shocking woman in the Strand--that adventuress. My dear, is it possible that you know her? Her name is in the mouth of everyone. She is quite notorious."

Instantly the room became full of voices, some talking loudly, some gently, but all praising Madame Sara. Even the men took her part; as to the women, they were unanimous about her charms and her genius.

In the midst of the commotion little Antonia burst into a flood of tears and left the room. Rowland followed her. What next occurred I cannot tell, but in the course of the morning I met Lady Kennedy.

"Well," she said," that child has won, as I knew she would. Madame Sara wishes to come here, and George says that Antonia's friend is to be invited. I shall be glad when the marriage is over and I can get out of this. It is really detestable that in the last days of my reign I should have to give that woman the *entrée* to the house."

She left me, and I wandered into the entrance hall. There I saw Rowland. He had a telegraph form in his hands, on which some words were written.

"Ah, Druce!" he said. "I am just sending a telegram to the station. What! Do you want to send one too?"

For I had seated myself by the table which held the telegraph forms.

"If you don't think I am taking too great a liberty, Rowland," I said, suddenly, "I should like to ask a friend of mine here for a day or two."

"Twenty friends, if you like, my dear Druce. What a man you are to apologize about such a trifle! Who is the special friend?"

"No less a person than Eric Vandeleur, the police-surgeon for Westminster."

"What! Vandeleur--the gayest, jolliest man I have ever met! Would he care to come?"

Rowland's eyes were sparkling with excitement.

"I think so; more especially if you will give me leave to say that you would welcome him."

"Tell him he shall have a thousand welcomes, the best room in the house, the best horse. Get him to come by all means, Druce."

Our two telegrams were sent off. In the course of the morning replies in the affirmative came to each.

That evening Madame Sara arrived. She came by the last train. The brougham was sent to meet her. She entered the house shortly before midnight. I was standing in the hall when she arrived, and I felt a momentary sense of pleasure when I saw her start as her eyes met mine. But she was not a woman to be caught off her guard. She approached me at once with outstretched hand and an eager voice.

"This is charming, Mr. Druce," she said. "I do not think anything pleases me more." Then she added, turning to Rowland, "Mr. Dixon Druce is a very old friend of mine."

Rowland gave e me a bewildered glance. Madame turned and began to talk to her hostess. Antonia was standing near one of the open drawing-rooms. She had on a soft dress of pale green silk. I had seldom seen a more graceful little creature. But the expression of her face disturbed me. It wore now the fascinated look of a bird when a snake attracts it. Could Madame Sara be the snake? Was Antonia afraid of this woman?

The next day Lady Kennedy came to me with a confidence.

"I am glad your police friend is coming," she said. "It will be safer."

"Vandeleur arrives at twelve o'clock," was my answer.

"Well, I am pleased. I like that woman less and less. I was amazed when she dared to call you her friend."

"Oh, we have met before on business," I answered, guardedly.

"You won't tell me anything further, Mr. Druce?"

"You must excuse me, Lady Kennedy."

"Her assurance is unbounded," continued the good lady. "She has brought a maid or nurse with her--a most extraordinary-looking woman. That, perhaps, is allowable; but she has also brought her black servant, an Arabian, who goes by the name of Achmed. I must say he is a picturesque creature with his quaint Oriental dress. He was all in flaming yellow this morning, and the embroidery on his jacket was worth a small fortune. But it is the daring of the woman that annoys me. She goes on as though she were somebody."

"She is a very emphatic somebody," I could not help replying. "London Society is at her feet."

"I only hope that Antonia will take her remedies and let her go. The woman has no welcome from me," said the indignant mistress of Rowland's Folly.

I did not see anything of Antonia that morning, and at the appointed time I went down to the station to meet Vandeleur. He arrived in high spirits, did not ask a question with regard to Antonia, received the information that Madame Sara was in the house with stolid silence, and seemed intent on the pleasures of the moment.

"Rowland's Folly!" he said, looking round him as we approached one of the finest houses in the whole of Yorkshire. "A folly truly, and yet a pleasant one, Druce, eh? I fancy," he added, with a slight smile, "that I am going to have a good time here."

"I hope you will disentangle a most tangled skein," was my reply.

He shrugged his shoulders. Suddenly his manner altered.

"Who is that woman?" he said, with a strain of anxiety quite apparent in his voice.

"Who?" I asked.

"That woman on the terrace in nurse's dress."

"I don't know. She has been brought here by Madame Sara--a sort of maid and nurse as well. I suppose poor little Antonia will be put under her charge."

"Don't let her see me, Druce, that's all. Ah, here is our host."

Vandeleur quickened his movements, and the next instant was shaking hands with Rowland.

The rest of the day passed without adventure. I did not see Antonia. She did not even appear at dinner. Rowland, however, assured me that she was taking necessary rest and would be all right on the morrow. He seemed inclined to be gracious to Madame Sara, and was annoyed at his sister's manner to their guest.

Soon after dinner, as I was standing in one of the smoking-rooms, I felt a light hand on my arm, and, turning, encountered the splendid pose and audacious, bright, defiant glance of Madame herself.

"Mr. Druce," she said, "just one moment. It is quite right that you and I should be plain with each other. I know the reason why you are here. You have come for the express purpose of spying upon me and spoiling what you consider my game. But understand, Mr. Druce, that there is danger to yourself when you interfere with the schemes of one like me. Forewarned is forearmed."

" FOREWARNED IS FOREARMED."

Someone came into the room and Madame left it.

The ball was but a week off, and preparations for the great event were taking place. Attached to the house at the left was a great room built for this purpose.

Rowland and I were walking down this room on a special morning; he was commenting on its architectural merits and telling me what band he intended to have in the musicians' gallery, when Antonia glided into the room.

"How pale you are, little Tonia!" he said.

This was his favorite name for her. He put his hand under her chin, raised her sweet, blushing face, and looked into her eyes.

"Ah, you want my answer. What a persistent little puss it is! You shall have your way, Tonia --yes, certainly. For you I will grant what has never been granted before. All the same, what will my lady say?"

He shrugged his shoulders.

"But you will let me wear them whether she is angry or not?" persisted Antonia.

"Yes, child, I have said it." She took his hand and raised it to her lips, then, with a curtsy, tripped out of the room.

"A rare, bright little bird," he said, turning to me. "Do you know, I feel that I have done an extraordinarily good thing for myself in securing little Antonia. No troublesome mamma in-law--no brothers and sisters, not my own and yet emphatically mine to consider--just the child herself. I am very happy and a very lucky fellow. I am glad my little girl has no past history. She is just her dear little, dainty self, no more and no less."

"What did she want with you now?" I asked.

"Little witch," he said, with a laugh. "The pearls--*the* pearls. She insists on wearing the great necklace on the night of the ball. Dear little girl. I can fancy how the baubles will gleam and shine on her fair throat."

I made no answer, but I was certain that little Antonia's request did not emanate from herself. I thought that I would search for Vandeleur and tell him of the circumstance, but the next remark of Rowland's nipped my project in the bud.

"By the way, your friend has promised to be back for dinner. He left here early this morning."

"Vandeleur?" I cried.

"Yes, he has gone to town. What a first-rate fellow he is!"

"He tells a good story," I answered.

"Capital. Who would suspect him of being the greatest criminal expert of the day? But, thank goodness, we have no need of his services at Rowland's Folly."

Late in the evening Vandeleur returned He entered the house just before dinner. I observed by the brightness of his eyes and the intense gravity of his manner that he was satisfied with himself. This in his case was always a good sign. At dinner he was his brightest self, courteous to everyone, and to Madame Sara in particular.

Late that night, as I was preparing to go to bed, he entered my room without knocking.

"Well, Druce," he said, "it is all right."

"All right!" I cried; "what do you mean?"

"You will soon know. The moment I saw that woman I had my suspicions. I was in town to-day making some very interesting inquiries. I am primed now on every point. Expect a *dénouement* of a startling character very soon, but be sure of one thing--however black appearances may be the little bride is safe, and so are the pearls."

He left me without waiting for my reply.

The next day passed, and the next. I seemed to live on tenter-hooks. Little Antonia was gay and bright like a bird. Madame's invitation had been extended by Lady Kennedy at Rowland's command to the day after the ball--little Antonia skipped when she heard it.

"I love her," said the girl.

More and more guests arrived---the days flew on wings--the evenings were lively. Madame was a power in herself. Vandeleur was another. These two, sworn foes at heart, aided and abetted each other to make things go brilliantly for the rest of the guests. Rowland was in the highest spirits.

At last the evening before the ball came and went. Vandeleur's *grand coup* had not come off. I retired to bed as usual. The night was a stormy one--rain rattled against the window-panes, the wind sighed and shuddered. I had just put out my candle and was about to seek forgetfulness in sleep when once again in his unceremonious fashion Vandeleur burst into my room.

"I want you at once, Druce, in the bed-room of Madame Sara's servant. Get into your clothes as fast as you possibly can and join me there."

He left the room as abruptly as he had entered it. I hastily dressed, and with stealthy steps, in the dead of night, to the accompaniment of the ever-increasing tempest, sought the room in question.

I found it brightly lighted; Vandeleur pacing the floor as though he himself were the very spirit of the storm; and, most astonishing sight of all, the nurse whom Madame Sara had brought to Rowland's Folly, and whose name I had never happened to hear, gagged and bound in a chair drawn into the centre of the room.

"So I think that is all, nurse," said Vandeleur, as I entered. "Pray take a chair, Druce. We quite understand each other, don't we, nurse, and the facts are wonderfully simple. Your name as entered in the archives of crime at Westminster is not as you have given out, Mary Jessop, but Rebecca Curt. You escaped from Portland prison on the night of November 30th, just a year ago. You could not have managed your escape but for the connivance of the lady in whose service you are now. Your crime was forgery, with a strong and very daring attempt at poisoning. Your victim was a harmless invalid lady. Your knowledge of crime, therefore, is what may be called extensive. There are yet eleven years of your sentence to run. You have doubtless served Madame Sara well--but perhaps you can serve me better. You know the consequence if you refuse, for I explained that to you frankly and clearly before this gentleman came into the room. Druce, will you oblige me--will you lock the door while I remove the gag from the prisoner's mouth?"

" WE QUITE UNDERSTAND EACH OTHER, DON'T WE, NURSE"

I hurried to obey. The woman breathed more freely when the gag was removed. Her face was a swarthy red all over. Her crooked eyes favoured us with many shifty glances.

"Now, then, have the goodness to begin, Rebecca Curt," said Vandeleur. "Tell us everything you can."

She swallowed hard, and said:--

"You have forced me----"

"We won't mind that part," interrupted Vandeleur. "The story, please, Mrs. Curt."

If looks could kill, Rebecca Curt would have killed Vandeleur then. He gave her in return a gentle, bland glance, and she started on her narrative.

"Madame knows a secret about Antonia Ripley."

"Of what nature?"

"It concerns her parentage."

"And that is?"

The woman hesitated and writhed.

"The names of her parents, please," said Vandeleur, in a voice cold as ice and hard as iron.

"Her father was Italian by birth."

"His name?"

"Count Gioletti. He was unhappily married, and stabbed his English wife in an access of jealousy when Antonia was three years old. He vas executed for the crime on the 20th of June, 18--. The child was adopted and taken out of the country by an English lady who was present in court--her name was Mrs. Studley. Madame Sara was also present. She was much interested in the trial, and had an interview afterwards with Mrs. Studley. It was arranged that Antonia should be called by the surname of Ripley--the name of an old relative of Mrs. Studley's--and that her real name and history were never to be told to her."

"I understand," said Vandeleur, gently. "This is of deep interest, is it not, Druce?"

I nodded, too much absorbed in watching the face of the woman to have time for words.

"But now," continued Vandeleur, "there are reasons why Madame should change her mind with regard to keeping the matter a close secret---is that not so, Mrs. Curt?"

"Yes," said Mrs. Curt.

"You will have the kindness to continue."

"Madame has an object--she blackmails the signora. She wants to get the signora completely into her power."

"Indeed! Is she succeeding?"

"Yes."

"How has she managed? Be very careful what you say, please."

"The mode is subtle--the young lady had a disfiguring mole or wart on her neck, just below the throat. Madame removed the mole."

"Quite a simple process, I doubt not," said Vandeleur, in a careless tone.

"Yes, it was done easily--I was present. The young lady was conducted into a chamber with a red light."

Vandeleur's extraordinary eyes suddenly leapt into fire. He took a chair and drew it so close to Mrs. Curt's that his face was within a foot or two of hers.

"Now, you will be very careful what you say," he remarked. "You know the consequence to yourself unless this narrative is absolutely reliable."

She began to tremble, but continued:--

"I was present at the operation. Not a single ray of ordinary light was allowed to penetrate. The patient was put under chloroform. The mole was removed. Afterwards Madame wrote something on her neck. The words were very small and neatly done--they formed a cross on the young lady's neck. Afterwards I heard what they were."

"Repeat them."

"I can't. You will know in the moment of victory."

"I choose to know now! A detective from my division at Westminster comes here early to-morrow morning--he brings hand-cuffs--and----"

"I will tell you,' interrupted the woman. "The words were these:--

"I am the daughter of Paolo Gioletti, who was executed for the murder of my mother, June 20th, 18--.'"

"How were the words written?"

"With nitrate of silver."

"Fiend!" muttered Vandeleur.

He jumped up and began to pace the room. I had never seen his face so black with ungovernable rage.

"You know what this means?" he said at last to me. "Nitrate of silver eats into the flesh and is permanent. Once exposed to the light the case is hopeless, and the helpless child becomes her own executioner."

The nurse looked up restlessly.

"The operation was performed in a room with a red light," she said, "and up to the present the words have not been seen. Unless the young lady exposes her neck to the blue rays of ordinary light they never will be. In order to give her a chance to keep her deadly secret Madame has had a large carbuncle on the deepest red cut and prepared. It is in the shape of a cross, and is suspended to a fine gold, almost invisible, thread. This, the signora is to wear when in full evening dress. It will keep in its place, for the back of the cross will be dusted with gum."

"But it cannot be Madame's aim to hide the fateful words," said Vandeleur. "You are concealing something, nurse."

Her face grew an ugly red. After a pause the following words came out with great reluctance:--

"The young lady wears the carbuncle as a reward."

"Ah," said Vandeleur, "now we are beginning to see daylight. As a reward for what?"

"Madame wants something which the signora can give her. It is a case of exchange; the carbuncle which hides the fatal secret is given in exchange for that which the signora can transfer to Madame."

"I understand at last," said Vandeleur. "Really, Druce, I feel myself privileged to say that of all the malevolent----" he broke off abruptly. "Never mind," he said, "we are keeping nurse. Nurse, you have answered all my questions with praiseworthy exactitude, but before you return to your well-earned slumbers I have one more piece of information to seek from you. Was it entirely by Miss Ripley's desire, or was it in any respect owing to Madame Sara's instigations, that the young lady is permitted to wear the pearl necklace on the night of the dance? You have, of course, nurse, heard of the pearl necklace?"

Rebecca Curt's face showed that she undoubtedly had.

"I see you are acquainted with that most interesting story. Now, answer my question. The request to wear the necklace to-morrow night was suggested by Madame, was it not?"

"Ah, yes--yes!" cried the woman, carried out of herself by sudden excitement. "It was to that point all else tended--all, all!"

"Thank you, that will do. You understand that from this day you are absolutely in my service. As long as you serve me faithfully you are safe."

"I will do my best, sir," she replied, in a modest tone, her eyes seeking the ground.

The moment we were alone Vandeleur turned to me.

"Things are simplifying themselves," he said.

"I fail to understand," was my answer. "I should say that complications, and alarming ones, abound."

"Nevertheless, I see my way clear. Druce, it is not good for you to be so long out of bed, but in order that you may repose soundly when you return to your room I will tell you frankly what my mode of operations will be to-morrow. The simplest plan would be to tell Rowland everything, but for various reasons that does not suit me. I take an interest in the little girl, and if she chooses to conceal her secret (at present, remember, she does not know it, but the poor child will certainly be told everything to-morrow) I don't intend to interfere. In the second place, I am anxious to lay a trap for Madame. Now, two things are evident. Madame Sara's object in coming here is to steal the pearls. Her plan is to terrify the little signora into giving them to her in order that the fiendish words written on the child's neck may not be seen. As the signora must wear a dress with a low neck to-morrow night, she can only hide the words by means of the red carbuncle. Madame will only give her the carbuncle if she, in exchange, gives Madame the pearls. You see?"

"I do," I answered, slowly.

He drew himself up to his slender height, and his eyes became full of suppressed laughter.

"The child's neck has been injured with nitrate of silver. Nevertheless, until it is exposed to the blue rays of light the ominous, fiendish words will not appear on her white throat. Once they do appear they will be indelible. Now, listen! Madame, with all her cunning, forgot something. To the action of nitrate of silver there is an antidote. This is nothing more or less than our old friend cyanide of potassium. To-morrow nurse, under my instructions, will take the little patient into a room carefully prepared with the hateful red light, and will bathe the neck just where the baleful words are written with a solution of cyanide of potassium. The nitrate of silver will then become neutralized and the letters will never come out."

"But the child will not know that. The terror of Madame's cruel story will be upon her, and she will exchange the pearls for the cross."

"I think not, for I shall be there to prevent it. Now, Druce, I have told you all that is necessary. Go to bed and sleep comfortably."

The next morning dawned dull and sullen, but the fierce storm of the night before was over. The ravages which had taken place, however, in the stately old park were very manifest, for trees had been torn up by their roots and some of the stateliest and largest of the oaks had been deprived of their best branches.

Little Miss Ripley did not appear at all that day. I was not surprised at her absence. The time had come when doubtless Madame found it necessary to divulge her awful scheme to the unhappy child. In the midst of that gay houseful of people no one specially missed her; even Rowland was engaged with many necessary matters, and had little time to devote to his future wife. The ballroom, decorated with real flowers, was a beautiful sight.

Vandeleur, our host, and I paced up and down the long room. Rowland was in great excitement, making many suggestions, altering this decoration and the other. The flowers were too profuse in one place, too scanty in another. The lights, too, were not bright enough.

"By all means have the ball-room well lighted," said Vandeleur. "In a room like this, so large, and with so many doors leading into passages and sitting-out rooms, it is well to have the light as brilliant as possible. You will forgive my suggestion, Mr. Rowland, when I say I speak entirely from the point of view of a man who has some acquaintance with the treacherous dealings of crime."

Rowland started.

"Are you afraid that an attempt will be made here to-night to steal the necklace?" he asked, suddenly.

"We won't talk of it," replied Vandeleur. "Act on my suggestion and you have nothing to fear."

Rowland shrugged his shoulders, and crossing the room gave some directions to several men who were putting in the final touches.

Nearly a hundred guests were expected to arrive from the surrounding country, and the house was as full as it could possibly hold. Rowland was to open the ball with little Antonia.

There was no late dinner that day, and as evening approached Vandeleur sought me.

"I say, Druce, dress as early as you can, and come down and meet me in our host's study."

I looked at him in astonishment, but did not question him. I saw that he was intensely excited. His face was cold and stern; it invariably wore that expression when he was most moved.

I hurried into my evening clothes and came down again. Vandeleur was standing in the study talking to Rowland. The guests were beginning to arrive. The musicians were tuning-up in the adjacent ball-room, and signs of hurry and festival pervaded the entire place. Rowland was in high spirits and looked very handsome. He and Vandeleur talked together, and I stood a little apart. Vandeleur was just about to make a light reply to one of our host's questions when we heard the swish of drapery in the passage outside, and little Antonia, dressed for her first ball, entered. She was in soft white lace, and her neck and arms were bare. The effect of her entrance was somewhat startling and would have arrested attention even were we not all especially interested in her. Her face, neck, and arms were nearly as white as her dress, her dark eyes were much dilated, and her soft black hair surrounded her small face like a shadow. In the midst of the whiteness a large red cross sparkled on her throat like living fire. Rowland uttered an exclamation and then stood still; as for Vandeleur and myself, we held our breath in suspense. What might not the next few minutes reveal?

It was the look on Antonia's face that aroused our fears. What ailed her? She came forward like one blind, or as one who walks in her sleep. One hand was held out slightly in advance, as though she meant to guide herself by the sense of touch. She certainly saw neither Vandeleur nor me, but when she got close to Rowland the blind expression left her eyes. She gave a sudden and exceedingly bitter cry, and ran forward, flinging herself into his arms.

"Kiss me once before we part for ever. Kiss me just once before we part," she said.

"My dear little one," I heard him answer, "what is the meaning of this? You are not well. There, Antonia, cease trembling. Before we part, my dear? But there is no thought of parting. Let me look at you, darling. Ah!"

He held her at arm's length and gazed at her critically.

"No girl could look sweeter, Antonia," he said, "and you have come now for the finishing touch---the beautiful pearls. But what is this, my dear? Why should you spoil your white neck with anything so incongruous? Let me remove it."

She put up her hand to her neck, thus covering the crimson cross. Then her wild eyes met Vandeleur's. She seemed to recognize his presence for the first time.

"You can safely remove it," he said to her, speaking in a semi-whisper.

Rowland gave him an astonished glance. His look seemed to say, "Leave us," but Vandeleur did not move.

"We must see this thing out," he said to me.

Meanwhile Rowland's arm encircled Antonia's neck, and his hand sought for the clasp of the narrow gold thread that held the cross in place.

"One moment," said Antonia.

She stepped back a pace; the trembling in her voice left it, it gathered strength, her fear gave way to dignity. This was the hour of her deepest humiliation, and yet she looked noble.

"My dearest," she said, "my kindest and best of friends. I had yielded to temptation, terror made me weak, the dread of losing you unnerved me, but I won't come to you charged with a sin on my conscience; I won't conceal anything from you. I know you won't wish me *now* to become your wife nevertheless, you shall know the truth."

"What do you mean, Antonia? What do your strange words signify? Are you mad?" said George Rowland.

"No, I wish I were; but I am no mate for you; I cannot bring dishonor to your honor. Madame said it could be hidden that this"--she touched the cross--"would hide it. For this I was to pay--yes, to pay a shameful price. I consented, for the terror was so cruel. But I--I came here and looked into your face and I could not do it. Madame shall have her blood-red cross back and you shall know all. You shall see." With a fierce gesture she tore the cross from her neck and flung it on the floor.

"The pearls for this," she cried; "the pearls were the price; but I would rather you knew. Take me up to the brightest light and you will see for yourself."

Rowland's face wore an expression impossible to fathom. The red cross lay on the floor; Antonia's eyes were fixed on his. She was no child to be humored; she was a woman and despair was driving her wild. When she said, "Take me up to the brightest light," he took her hand without a word and led her to where the full rays of a powerful electric light turned the place into day.

"Look!" cried Antonia, "look! Madame wrote it here--here."

She pointed to her throat.

"The words are hidden, but this light will soon cause them to appear. You will see for yourself, you will know the truth. At last you will understand who I really am."

There was silence for a few minutes. Antonia kept pointing to her neck. Rowland's eyes were fixed upon it. After a breathless period of agony Vandeleur stepped forward.

"Miss Antonia," he cried, "you have suffered enough. I am in a position to relieve your terrors. You little guessed, Rowland, that for the last few days I have taken an extreme liberty with regard to you. I have been in your house simply and solely in the exercise of my professional qualities. In the exercise of my manifest duties I came across a ghastly secret. Miss Antonia was to be subjected to a cruel ordeal. Madame Sara, for reasons of her own, had invented one of the most

73

fiendish plots it has ever been my unhappy lot to come across. But I have been in time. Miss Antonia, you need fear nothing. Your neck contains no ghastly secret. Listen! I have saved you. The nurse whom Madame believed to be devoted to her service considered it best for prudential reasons to transfer herself to me. Under my directions she bathed your neck to-day with a preparation of cyanide of potassium. You do not know what that is, but it is a chemical preparation which neutralizes the effect of what that horrible woman has done. You have nothing to fear--your secret lies buried beneath your white skin."

"But what is the mystery?" said Rowland. "Your actions, Antonia, and your words, Vandeleur, are enough to drive a man mad. What is it all about? I will know." "Miss Ripley can tell you or not, as she pleases," replied Vandeleur. "The unhappy child was to be blackmailed, Madame Sara's object being to secure the pearl necklace worth a King's ransom. The cross was to be given in exchange for the necklace. That was her aim, but she is defeated. Ask me no questions, sir. If this young lady chooses to tell you, well and good, but if not the secret is her own."

Vandeleur bowed and backed towards me.

"The secret is mine," cried Antonia, "but it also shall be yours, George. I will not be your wife with this ghastly thing between us. You may never speak to me again, but you shall know all the truth."

"Upon my word, a brave girl, and I respect her," whispered Vandeleur. "Come, Druce, our work so far as Miss Antonia is concerned is finished."

We left the room.

"Now to see Madame Sara," continued my friend. "We will go to her rooms. Walls have ears in her case; she doubtless knows the whole *dénouement* already; but we will find her at once, she can scarcely have escaped yet."

He flew upstairs. I followed him. We went from one corridor to another. At last we found Madame's apartments. Her bedroom door stood wide open. Rebecca Curt was standing in the middle of the room. Madame herself was nowhere to be seen, but there was every sign of hurried departure.

"Where is Madame Sara?" inquired Vandeleur, in a peremptory voice.

Rebecca Curt shrugged her shoulders.

"Has she gone down? Is she in the ball-room? Speak!" said Vandeleur.

The nurse gave another shrug.

"I only know that Achmed the Arabian rushed in here a few minutes ago," was her answer. "He was excited. He said something to Madame. I think he had been listening-- eavesdropping, you call it. Madame was convulsed with rage. She thrust a few things together and she's gone. Perhaps you can catch her."

Vandeleur's face turned white.

"I'll have a try," he said. "Don't keep me, Druce."

He rushed away. I don't know what immediate steps he took, but he did not return to Rowland's Folly. Neither was Madame Sara captured.

But notwithstanding her escape and her meditated crime, notwithstanding little Antonia's hour of terror, the ball went on merrily, and the bride-elect opened it with her future husband. On her fair neck gleamed the pearls, lovely in their soft luster. What she told Rowland was never known; how he took the news is a secret between Antonia and himself. But one thing is certain: no one was more gallant in his conduct, more ardent in his glances of love, than was the master of Rowland's Folly that night. They were married on the day fixed, and Madame Sara was defeated.

III. *The face of the abbot*

IF Madame Sara had one prerogative more than another it was that of taking people unawares. When least expected she would spring a mine at your feet, engulf you in a most horrible danger, stab you in the dark, or injure you through your best friend; in short, this dangerous woman was likely to become the terror of London if steps were not soon taken to place her in such confinement that her genius could no longer assert itself.

Months went by after my last adventure. Once again my fears slumbered. Madame Sara's was not the first name that I thought of when I awoke in the morning, nor the last to visit my dreams at night. Absorbed in my profession, I had little time to waste upon her. After all, I made up my mind, she might have left London; she might have carried her machinations, her cruelties, and her genius elsewhere.

That such was not the case this story quickly shows.

The matter which brought Madame Sara once again to the fore began in the following way.

On the 17th of July, 1900, I received a letter; it ran as follows:--

"23, West Terrace,

"Charlton Road, Putney.

"Dear Mr. Druce,--

I am in considerable difficulty and am writing to beg for your advice. My father died a fortnight ago at his castle in Portugal, leaving me his heiress. His brother-in-law, who lived there with him, arrived in London yesterday and came to see me, bringing me full details of my father's death. These are in the last degree mysterious and terrifying. There are also a lot of business affairs to arrange. I know little about business and should greatly value your advice on the whole situation. Can you come here and see me to-morrow at three o'clock? Senhor de Castro, my uncle, my mother's brother, will be here, and I should like you to meet him. If you can come I shall be very grateful.--Yours sincerely,

"Helen Sherwood."

I replied to this letter by telegram:---

"Will be with you at three tomorrow."

Helen Sherwood was an old friend of mine; that is, I had known her since she was a child. She was now about twenty-three years of age, and was engaged to a certain Godfrey Despard, one of the best fellows I ever met. Despard was employed in a merchant's office in Shanghai, and the chance of immediate marriage was small. Nevertheless, the young people were determined to be true to each other and to wait that turn in the tide which comes to most people who watch for it.

Helen's life had been a sad one. Her mother, a Portuguese lady of good family, had died at her birth; her father, Henry Sherwood, had gone to Lisbon in 1860 as one of the Under-Secretaries to the Embassy and never cared to return to England. After the death of his wife he had lived as an eccentric recluse. When Helen was three years old he had sent her home, and she had been brought up by a maiden aunt of her father's, who had never understood the impulsive, eager girl, and had treated her with a rare want of sympathy. This woman had died when her young charge was sixteen years of age. She had left no money behind her, and, as her father declined to devote one penny to his daughter's maintenance, Helen had to face the world before her education was finished. But her character was full of spirit and determination. She stayed on at school as pupil teacher, and afterwards supported herself by her attainments. She was a good linguist, a clever musician, and had one of the most charming voices I ever heard in an amateur. When this story opens she was earning a comfortable independence, and was even saving a little money for that distant date when she would marry the man she loved.

Meanwhile Sherwood's career was an extraordinary one. He had an extreme stroke of fortune in drawing the first prize of the Grand Christmas State Lottery in Lisbon, amounting to one hundred and fifty million reis, representing in English money thirty thousand pounds. With this sum he bought an old castle in the Estrella Mountains, and, accompanied by his wife's brother, a certain Petro de Castro, went there to live. He was hated by his fellow-men and, with the exception of De Castro, he had no friends. The old castle was said to be of extraordinary beauty, and was known as Castello Mondego. It was situated some twenty miles beyond the old Portuguese town of Coimbra. The historical accounts of the place were full of interest, and its situation was marvelously romantic, being built on the heights above the Mondego River. The castle dated from the twelfth century, and had seen brave and violent deeds. It was supposed to be haunted by an old monk who was said to have been murdered there, but within living memory no one had seen him. At least, so Helen had informed me.

Punctually at three o'clock on the following day I found myself at West Terrace, and was shown into my young friend's pretty little sitting-room.

"How kind of you to come, Mr. Druce!" she said. "May I introduce you to my uncle, Senor de Castro?"

The Senor, a fine-looking man, who spoke English remarkably well, bowed, gave a gracious smile, and immediately entered into conversation. His face had strong features; his beard was iron-grey, so also were his hair and moustache. He was slightly bald about the temples. I imagined him to be a man about forty-five years of age.

"Now," said Helen, after we had talked to each other for a few minutes, "perhaps, Uncle Petro, you will explain to Mr. Druce what has happened."

As she spoke I noticed that her face was very pale and that her lips slightly trembled.

"It is a painful story," said the Portuguese, "most horrible and inexplicable."

I prepared myself to listen, and he continued:--

"For the last few months my dear friend had been troubled in his mind. The reason appeared to me extraordinary. I knew that Sherwood was eccentric, but he was also matter-of-fact, and I should have thought him the last man who would be likely to be a prey to nervous terrors. Nevertheless, such was the case. The old castle has the reputation of being haunted, and the apparition that is supposed to trouble Mondego is that of a ghastly white face that is now and then seen at night peering out through some of the windows or one of the embrasures of the battlements surrounding the courtyard. It is said to be the shade of an abbot who was foully murdered there by a Castilian nobleman who owned the castle a hundred years ago.

"It was late in April of this year when my brother-in-law first declared that he saw the apparition. I shall never forget his terror. He came to me in my room, woke me, and pointed out the embrasure where he had seen it. He described it as a black figure leaning out of a window, with an appallingly horrible white face, with wide-open eyes apparently staring at nothing. I argued with him and tried to appeal to his common sense, and did everything in my power to bring him to reason, but without avail. I he terror grew worse and worse. He could think and talk of nothing else, and, to make matters worse, he collected all the old literature he could find bearing on the legend. This he would read, and repeat the ghastly information to me at meal times. I began to fear that his mind would become affected, and three weeks ago I persuaded him to come away with me for a change to Lisbon. He agreed, but the very night before we were to leave I was awakened in the small hours by hearing an awful cry, followed by another, and then the sound of my own name. I ran out into the courtyard and looked up at the battlements. There I saw, to my horror, my brother-in-law rushing along the edge, screaming as though in extreme terror, and evidently imagining that he was pursued by something. The next moment he dashed headlong down a hundred feet on to the flagstones by my side, dying instantaneously. Now comes the most horrible part. As I glanced up I saw, and I swear it with as much certainty as I am now speaking to you, a black figure leaning out over the battlement exactly at the spot from which he had fallen--a figure with a ghastly white face, which stared straight down at me. The moon was full, and gave the face a clearness that was unmistakable. It was large, round, and smooth, white with a whiteness I had never seen on human face, with eyes widely open, and a fixed stare; the face was rigid and tense; the mouth shut and drawn at the corners. Fleeting as the glance was, for it vanished almost the next moment, I shall never forget it. It is indelibly imprinted on my memory."

He ceased speaking.

From my long and constant contact with men and their affairs, I knew at once that what De Castro had just said instantly raised the whole matter out of the commonplace; true or untrue, real or false, serious issues were at stake.

"Who else was in the castle that night?" I asked

"No one," was his instant reply. "Not even old Gonsalves, our one man-servant. He had gone to visit his people in the mountains about ten miles off. We were absolutely alone."

"You know Mr. Sherwood's affairs pretty well?" I went on. "On the supposition of trickery, could there be any motive that you know of for anyone to play such a ghastly trick?"

"Absolutely none."

"You never saw the apparition before this occasion?"

"Never."

"And what were your next steps?"

"There was nothing to be done except to carry poor Sherwood indoors. He was buried on the following day. I made every effort to have a systematic inquiry set on foot, but the castle is in a remote spot and the authorities are slow to move. The Portuguese doctor gave his sanction to the burial after a formal inquiry. Deceased was testified as having committed suicide while temporarily insane, but to investigate the apparition they absolutely declined."

"And now," I said, "will you tell me what you can with regard to the disposition of the property?"

"The will is a very remarkable one," replied De Castro. "Senor Sousa, my brother-in-law's lawyer, holds it. Sherwood died a much richer man than I had any idea of. This was owing to some very successful speculations. The real and personal estate amounts to seventy thousand pounds, but the terms of the will are eccentric. Henry Sherwood's passionate affection for the old castle was quite morbid, and the gist of the conditions of the will is this: Helen is to live on the property, and if she does, and as long as she does, she is to receive the full interest on forty thousand pounds, which is now invested in good English securities. Failing this condition, the property is to be sold, and the said forty thousand pounds is to go to a Portuguese charity in Lisbon. I also have a personal interest in the will. This I knew from Sherwood himself He told me that his firm intention was to retain the castle in the family for his daughter, and for her son if she married. He earnestly begged of me to promote his wishes in the event of his dying. I was not to leave a stone unturned to persuade Helen to live at the castle, and in order to ensure my carrying out his wishes he bequeathed to me the sum of ten thousand pounds provided Helen lives at Castello Mondego. If she does not do so I lose the money. Hence my presence here and my own personal anxiety to clear up the mystery of my friend's death, and to see my niece installed as owner of the most lovely and romantic property in the Peninsula. It has, of course, been my duty to give a true account of the mystery surrounding my unhappy brother-in-law's death, and I sincerely trust that a solution to this terrible mystery will be found, and that Helen will enter into her beautiful possessions with all confidence."

"The terms of the will are truly eccentric," I said. Then turning to Helen I added:--

"Surely you can have no fear in living at Castello Mondego when it would be the means of bringing about the desire of your heart?"

"Does that mean that you are engaged to be married, Helen?" asked De Castro.

"It does," she replied. Then she turned to me. "I am only human, and a woman. I could not live at Castello Mondego with this mystery unexplained; but I am willing to take every step--yes, *every* step, to find out the truth."

"Let me think over the case," I said, after a pause. "Perhaps I may be able to devise some plan for clearing up this unaccountable matter. There is no man in the whole of London better fitted to grapple with the mystery than I, for it is, so to speak, my profession."

"You will please see in me your hearty collaborator, Mr. Druce," said Senor de Castro.

"When do you propose to return to Portugal?" I asked.

"As soon as I possibly can."

Where are you staying now?"

"At the Cecil."

He stood up as he spoke.

"I am sorry to have to run away," he said. "I promised to meet a friend, a lady, in half an hour from now. She is a very busy woman, and I must not keep her waiting."

His words were commonplace enough, but I noticed a queer change in his face. His eyes grew full of eagerness, and yet--was it possible?--a curious fear seemed also to fill them. He shook hands with Helen, bowed to me, and hurriedly left the room.

"I wonder whom he is going to meet," she said, glancing out of the window and watching his figure as he walked down the street. "He told me when he first came that he had an interview pending of a very important character. But, there, I must not keep you, Mr. Druce; you are also a very busy man. Before you go, however, do tell me what you think of the whole thing. I certainly cannot live at the castle while that ghastly face is unexplained; but at the same time I do not wish to give up the property."

"You shall live there, enjoy the property, and be happy," I answered. "I will think over everything; I am certain we shall see a way out of the mystery."

I wrung her hand and hurried away.

During the remainder of the evening this extraordinary case occupied my thoughts to the exclusion of almost everything else. I made up my mind to take it up, to set every inquiry on foot, and, above all things, to ascertain if there was a physical reason for the apparition's appearance; in short, if Mr. Sherwood's awful death was for the benefit of any living person. But I must confess that, think as I would, I could not see the slightest daylight until I remembered the curious expression of De Castro's face when he spoke of his appointment with a lady. The man had undoubtedly his weak point; he had his own private personal fear. What was its nature?

I made a note of the circumstance and determined to speak to Vandeleur about it when I had a chance.

The next morning one of the directors of our agency called. He and I had a long talk over business matters, and when he was leaving he asked me when I wished to take my holiday.

"If you like to go away for a fortnight or three weeks, now is your time," was his final remark.

I answered without a moment's hesitation that I should wish to go to Portugal, and would take advantage of the leave of absence which he offered me.

Now, it had never occurred to me to think of visiting Portugal until that moment; but so strongly did the idea now take possession of me that I went at once to the Cecil and had an interview with De Castro. I told him that I could not fulfil my promise to Miss Sherwood without being on the spot, and I should therefore accompany him when he returned to Lisbon. His face expressed genuine delight, and before we parted we arranged to meet at Charing Cross on the morning after the morrow. I then hastened to Putney to inform Helen Sherwood of my intention.

To my surprise I saw her busy placing different articles of her wardrobe in a large trunk which occupied the place of honor in the centre of the little sitting-room.

"What are you doing?" I cried.

She colored.

"You must not scold me," she said. "There is only one thing to do, and I made up my mind this morning to do it. The day after to-morrow I am going to Lisbon. I mean to investigate the mystery for myself."

"You are a good, brave girl," I cried. "But listen, Helen; it is not necessary."

I then told her that I had unexpectedly obtained a few weeks' holiday and that I intended to devote the time to her service.

"Better and better," she cried. "I go with you. Nothing could have been planned more advantageously for me."

"What put the idea into your head?" I asked.

"It isn't my own," she said. "I spent a dreadful night, and this morning, soon after ten o'clock, I had an unexpected visitor. She is not a stranger to me, although I have never mentioned her name. She is known as Madame Sara, and is--"

"My dear Helen!" I cried. "You don't mean to tell me you know that woman? She is one of the most unscrupulous in the whole of London. You must have nothing to do with her--nothing whatever."

Helen opened her eyes to their widest extent.

"You misjudge Madame Sara," she said. "I have known her for the last few years, and she has been a most kind friend to me. She has got me more than one good post as teacher, and I have always felt a warm admiration for her. She is, beyond doubt, the most unselfish woman I ever met."

I shook my head.

"You will not get me to alter my opinion of her," continued Helen. "Think of her kindness in calling to see me to-day. She drove here this morning just because she happened to see my uncle, Petro de Castro, yesterday. She has known him, too, for some time. She had a talk with him about me, and he told her all about the strange will. She was immensely interested, and said that it was imperative for me to investigate the matter myself. She spoke in the most sensible way, and said finally that she would not leave me until I had promised to go to Portugal to visit the castle, and in my own person to unearth the mystery. I promised her and felt she was right. I am keeping my word."

When Helen had done speaking I remained silent. I could scarcely describe the strange sensation which visited me. Was it possible that the fear which I had seen so strongly depicted on De Castro's face was caused by Madame Sara? Was the mystery in the old Portuguese castle also connected with this terrible woman? If so, what dreadful revelations might not be before us! Helen was not the first innocent girl who believed in Madame, and not the first whose life was threatened.

"Why don't you speak, Mr. Druce?" she asked me at last. "What are you thinking of?"

"I would rather not say what I am thinking of," I answered; "but I am very glad of one thing, and that is that I am going with you."

"You are my kindest, best friend," she said; "and now I will tell you one thing more. Madame said that the fact of your being one of the party put all danger out of the case so far as I was concerned, for she knew you to be the cleverest man she ever met."

"Ah!" I replied, slowly, "there is a cleverer man than I, and his name is Eric Vandeleur. Did she happen to speak of him?"

"No. Who is he? I have never heard of him."

"I will tell you some day," I replied, " but not now."

I rose, bade her a hasty good-bye, and went straight to Vandeleur's rooms.

Whatever happened, I had made up my mind to consult him in the matter. He was out when I called, but I left a note, and he came round to my place in the course of the evening.

In less than a quarter of an hour I put him in possession of all the facts. He received my story in silence.

"Well!" I cried at last. "What do you think?"

"There is but one conclusion, Druce," was his reply. "There is a motive in this mystery--method in this madness. Madame is mixed up in it. That being the case, anything supernatural is out of the question. I am sorry Miss Sherwood is going to Lisbon, but the fact that you are going too may be her protection. Beyond doubt her life is in danger. Well, you must do your best, and forewarned is forearmed. I should like to go with you, but I cannot. Perhaps I may do more good here watching the arch-fiend who is pulling the strings."

De Castro took the information quietly that his niece was about to accompany us.

"Women are strange creatures," he said. "Who would suppose that a delicate girl would subject herself to the nervous terrors she must undergo in the castle? Well, let her come--it may be best, and my friend, the lady about whom I spoke to you, recommended it."

"You mean Madame Sara?" I said.

"' YOU MEAN MADAME SARA?' I SAID."

"Ah!" he answered, with a start. "Do you know her?"

"Slightly," I replied, in a guarded tone. Then I turned the conversation.

Our journey took place without adventure, and when we got to Lisbon we put up at Durrand's Hotel.

On the afternoon of that same day we went to interview Manuel Sousa, the lawyer who had charge of Mr.

Sherwood's affairs. His office was in the Rue do Rio Janeiro. He was a short, bright-eyed little man, having every appearance of honesty and ability. He received us affably and looked with much interest at Helen Sherwood, whose calm, brave face and English appearance impressed him favorably.

"So you have come all this long way, Senora," he said, "to investigate the mystery of your poor father's death? Be assured I will do everything in my power to help you. And now you would all like to see the documents and papers. Here they are at your service."

He opened a tin box and lifted out a pile of papers. Helen went up to one of the windows.

"I don't understand Portuguese," she said. "You will examine them for me, won't you Uncle Petro, and you also, Mr. Druce?"

I had a sufficient knowledge of Portuguese to be able to read the will, and I quickly discovered that De Castro's account of it was quite correct.

"Is it your intention to go to Castello Mondego?" asked the lawyer, when our interview was coming to an end.

"I can answer for myself that I intend to go," I replied.

"It will give me great pleasure to take Mr. Druce to that romantic spot," said De Castro.

"And I go with you," cried Helen.

"My dear, dear young lady," said the lawyer, a flicker of concern crossing his bright eyes, "is that necessary? You will find the castle very lonely and not prepared for the reception of a lady."

"Even so, I have come all this long way to visit it," replied Helen. "I go with my friend, Mr. Druce, and with my uncle, and so far as I am concerned the sooner we get there the better."

The lawyer held up his hands. "I wouldn't sleep in that place," he exclaimed, "for twenty *contos* of *reis*."

"Then you really believe in the apparition?" I said. "You think it is supernatural?"

He involuntarily crossed himself.

"The tale is an old one," he said. " It has been known for a hundred years that the castle is haunted by a monk who was treacherously murdered there. That is the reason, Miss Sherwood, why your father got it so cheap."

"Supernatural or not, I must get to the bottom of the thing," she said, in a low voice.

De Castro jumped up, an impatient expression crossing his face.

"If you don't want me for the present, Druce," he said. "I have some business of my own that I wish to attend to."

He left the office, and Helen and I were about to follow him when Senor Sousa suddenly addressed me.

"By the way, Mr. Druce, I am given to understand that you are from the Solvency Inquiry Agency of London. I know that great business well; I presume, therefore, that matters of much interest depend upon this inquiry? "

"The interests are great," I replied, "but are in no way connected with my business. My motive in coming here is due to friendship. This young lady is engaged to be married to a special friend of mine, and I have known her personally from her childhood. If we can clear up the present mystery, Helen Sherwood's marriage can take place at once. If, on the other hand, that terror which hangs over Castello Mondego is so overpowering that Miss Sherwood cannot make up her mind to live there, a long separation awaits the young pair. I have answered your question, Senor Sousa; will you, on your part, answer mine?"

"Certainly," he replied. His face looked keenly interested, and from time to time he glanced from Helen to me.

"Are you aware of the existence of any motive which would induce someone to personate the apparition and so bring about Mr. Sherwood's death?"

"I know of no such motive, my dear sir. Senor de Castro will come into ten thousand pounds provided, and only provided, Miss Sherwood takes possession of the property. He is the one and only person who benefits under the will, except Miss Sherwood herself."

"We must, of course, exclude Senor de Castro," I answered. "His conduct has been most honorable in the matter throughout; he might have been tempted to suppress the story of the ghost, which would have been to his obvious advantage. Is there no one else whom you can possibly suspect?"

"No one--absolutely no one."

"Very well; my course is clear. I have come here to get an explanation of the mystery. When it is explained Miss Sherwood will take possession of the castle."

94

"And should you fail, sir? Ghosts have a way of suppressing themselves when most earnestly desired to put in an appearance."

"I don't anticipate failure, Senor Sousa, and I mean to go to the castle immediately."

"We are a superstitious race," he replied, "and I would not go there for any money you liked to offer me."

"I am an Englishman, and this lady is English on her father's side. We do not easily abandon a problem when we set to work to solve it."

"What do you think of it all?" asked Helen of me, when we found ourselves soon afterwards in the quaint, old-world streets.

"Think!" I answered. "Our course is clear. We have got to discover the motive. There must be a motive. There was someone who had a grudge against the old man, and who wished to terrify him out of the world. As to believing that the apparition is supernatural, I decline even to allow myself to consider it."

"Heaven grant that you may be right," she answered; " but I must say a strange and Most unaccountable terror oppresses me whenever I conjure un that ghastly face."

"And yet you have the courage to go to the castle!"

"It is a case of duty, not of courage, Mr. Druce."

For the rest of that day I thought over the whole problem, looking at it from every point of view, trying to gaze at it with fresh eyes, endeavoring to discover the indiscoverable--the motive. There must be a motive. We should find it at the castle. We would go there on the morrow. But, no; undue haste was unnecessary. It might be well for me, helped as I should be by my own agency, a branch of which was to be found in Lisbon, to discover amongst the late Mr. Sherwood's acquaintances, friends, or relatives the motive that I wanted. My agents set to work for me, but though they did their utmost no discovery of the least value was found, and at the end of a week I told De Castro and Helen that I was ready to start.

"We will go early to-morrow morning," I said. "You must make all your preparations, Helen. It will take us the day to reach Castello Mondego. I hope that our work may be completed there and that we may be back again in Lisbon within the week."

Helen's face lit up with a smile of genuine delight.

"The inaction of the last week has been terribly trying," she said. "But now that we are really going to get near the thing I feel quite cheerful."

"Your courage fills me with admiration," I could not help saying, and then I went out to make certain purchases. Amongst these were three revolvers--one for Helen, one for De Castro, and one for myself.

Afterwards I had an interview with Sousa, and took him as far as I could into my confidence.

"The danger of the supernatural is not worth considering," I said, "but the danger of treachery, of unknown motives, is considerable. I do not deny this fact for a moment. In case you get no tidings of us, come yourself or send some one to the castle within a week."

"This letter came for you by the last post," said Sousa, and he handed me one from Vandeleur.

I opened it and read as follows:--

"I met Madame Sara a week ago at the house of a friend. I spoke to her about Castello Mondego. She admitted that she was interested in it, that she knew Miss Sherwood, and hoped when she had taken possession to visit her in that romantic spot. I inquired further if she was aware of the contents of the strange will. She said she had heard of it. Her manner was perfectly frank, but I saw that she was uneasy. She took the first opportunity of leaving the house, and on making inquiries I hear that she left London by the first train this morning, *en route* for the Continent. These facts may mean a great deal, and I should advise you to be more than ever on your guard."

I put the letter into my pocket, got Sousa to promise all that was necessary, and went away.

At an early hour the following morning we left Rocio Station for Coimbra, and it was nearly seven in the evening when we finally came to the end of our railway journey and entered a light wagonette drawn by two powerful bay stallions for our twenty-mile drive to the castle.

The scenery as we approached the spurs of the Estrella was magnificent beyond description, and as I gazed up at the great peaks, now bathed in the purples and golds of the sunset, the magic and mystery of our strange mission became tenfold intensified. Presently the steep ascent began along a winding road between high walls that shut out our view, and by the time we reached the castle it was too dark to form any idea of its special features.

97

De Castro had already sent word of our probable arrival, and when we rang the bell at the old castle a phlegmatic-looking man opened the door for us.

"Ah, Gonsalves," cried De Castro, "here we are! I trust you have provided comfortable beds and a good meal, for we are all as hungry as hawks."

The old man shrugged his shoulders, raised his beetle-brows a trifle, and fixed his eyes on Helen with some astonishment. He muttered, in a Portuguese dialect which I did not in the least comprehend, something to De Castro who professed himself satisfied. Then he, said something further, and I noticed the face of my Portuguese friend turn pale.

"Gonsalves saw the specter three nights ago," he remarked, turning to me. "It was leaning as usual out of one of the windows of the north-west turret. But, come; we must not terrify ourselves the moment we enter your future home, Niece Helen. You are doubtless hungry. Shall we go to the banqueting-hall?"

The supper prepared for us was not appetizing, consisting of some miserable goat chops, and in the great hall, dimly lighted by a few candles in silver sconces, we could scarcely see each other's faces. As supper was coming to an end I made a suggestion.

"We have come here," I said, "on a serious matter. We propose to start an investigation of a very grave character. It is well known that ghosts prefer to reveal themselves to one man or woman alone, and not to a company. I propose, therefore, that we three should occupy rooms as far as possible each from the other in the castle, and that the windows of our three bedrooms should command the centre square."

De Castro shrugged his shoulders and a look of dismay spread for a moment over his face; but Helen fixed her great eyes on mine, her lips moved slightly as though she would speak, then she pulled herself together.

"You are right, Mr. Druce," she said. "Having come on this inquiry, we must fear nothing."

"Well, come at once, and we will choose our bedrooms. You as the lady shall have the first choice."

De Castro called Gonsalves, who appeared holding a lantern in his hand. A few words were said to the man in his own dialect, and he led the way, going up many stone stairs, down many others, and at last he flung open a huge oak door and we found ourselves in a vast chamber with five windows, all mullioned and sunk in deep recesses. On the floor was a heavy carpet. A four-post bed-head with velvet hangings was in a recess. The rest of the furniture was antique and massive, nearly black with age, but relieved by brass mountings, which, strange to say, were bright as though they had recently been rubbed.

"This was poor Sherwood's own bedroom," said De Castro. "Do you mind sleeping here?"

He turned to Helen.

"No, I should like it," she replied, emphatically.

"I am glad that this is your choice," he said, "for I don't believe, although I am a man and you are a woman, that I could myself endure this room. It was here I watched by his dead body. Ah, poor fellow, I loved him well."

"We won't talk of memories tonight," said Helen. "I am very tired, and I believe I shall sleep. Strange as it may sound, I am not afraid. Mr. Druce, where will you locate yourself? I should like, at least, to know what room you will be in."

I smiled at her. Her bravery astonished me. I selected a room at right angles to Helen's. Standing in one of her windows she could, if necessary, get a glimpse of me if I were to stand in one of mine.

De Castro chose a room equally far away from Helen's on the other side. We then both bade the girl good-night.

"I hate to leave her so far from help," I said, glancing at De Castro.

"Nothing will happen," he replied. "I can guarantee that. I am dead tired; the moment I lay my head on my pillow, ghost or no ghost, I shall sleep till morning."

He hurried off to his own room.

The chamber that I had selected was vast, lofty, and might have accommodated twenty people. I must have been more tired even than I knew, for I fell asleep when my head touched the pillow.

When I awoke it was dawn, and, eager to see my surroundings by the light of day, I sprang up, dressed, and went down to the courtyard. Three sides of this court were formed by the castle buildings, but along the fourth ran a low balustrade of stone. I sauntered towards it. I shall never forget the loveliness of the scene that met my eyes. I stood upon what was practically a terrace--a mere shelf on the scarping of rock on the side of a dizzy cliff that went down below me a sheer two thousand feet. The Mondego River ran with a swift rushing noise at the foot of the gorge, although at the height at which I stood it looked more like a thread of silver than any thing else. Towering straight in front of me, solemnly up into the heavens, stood the great peak of the *Serra da Estrella*, from which in the rosy sunrise the morning clouds were rolling into gigantic white wreaths. Behind me was the great irregular pile of the castle, with its battlements, turrets, and cupolas, hoar and grey with the weight of centuries, but now transfigured and bathed in the golden light. I had just turned lo glance at them when I saw De Castro approaching me.

"Surely," I said, "there never was such a beautiful place in the world before! We can never let it go out of the family. Helen shall live here."

De Castro came close to me; he took my arm, and pointed to a spot on the stone flags.

"On this very spot her father fell from the battlements above," he said, slowly.

I shuddered, and all pleasant thoughts were instantly dispelled by the memory of that hideous tragedy and the work we had still to do. It seemed impossible in this radiant, living sunlight to realize the horror that these walls had contained, and might still contain. At some of these very windows the ghastly face had appeared.

Helen, De Castro, and I spent the whole day exploring the castle. We went from dungeons to turrets, and made elaborate plans for alternate nightly vigils. One of the first things that I insisted on was that Gonsalves should not sleep in the castle at night. This was easily arranged, the old man having friends in the neighboring village. Thus the only people in the castle after nightfall would be De Castro, Helen, and myself.

After we had locked old Gonsalves out and had raised the portcullis, we again went the complete round of the entire place. Thus we ensured that no one else could be hiding in the precincts. Finally we placed across every entrance thin silken threads which would be broken if anyone attempted to pass them.

Helen was extremely anxious that the night should be divided into three portions, and that she should share the vigils; but this both De Castro and I prohibited.

"At least for to-night," I said. "Sleep soundly; trust the matter to us. Believe me, this will be best. All arrangements are made. Your uncle will patrol until one o'clock in the morning, then I will go on duty."

This plan was evidently most repugnant to her, and when De Castro left the room she came up and began to plead with me.

"I have a strange and overpowering sensation of terror," she said. "Fight as I will, I cannot get rid of it. I would much rather be up than in that terrible room. I slept last night because I was too weary to do anything else, but I am wakeful to-night, and I shall not close my eyes. Let me share your watch at least. Let us pace the courtyard side by side."

"No," I answered, "that would not do. If two of us are together the ghost, or whatever human being poses as the ghost, will not dare to put in an appearance. We must abide by our terrible mission, Helen; each must watch alone. You will go to bed now, like a good girl, and to-morrow night, if we have not then discovered anything, you will be allowed to take your share in the night watch."

"Very well," she answered.

She sighed impatiently, and after a moment she said:--

"I have a premonition that something will happen tonight. As a rule my premonitions come right."

I made no answer, but I could not help giving her a startled glance. It is one thing to be devoid of ghostly terrors when living in practical London, surrounded by the world and the ways of men, but it is another thing to be proof against the strange terror which visits all human beings more or less when they are alone, when it is night, when the heart beats low. Then we are apt to have distorted visions, our mental equilibrium is upset, and we fear we know not what.

Helen and I knew that there was something to fear, and as our eyes met we dared not speak of what was uppermost in our thoughts. I could not find De Castro, and presumed that he had taken up his watch without further ado. I therefore retired to my own room and prepared to sleep. But the wakefulness which had seized Helen was also mine, for when the Portuguese entered my bedroom at one o'clock I was wide awake.

"You have seen nothing?" I said to him.

"Nothing," he answered, cheerfully. "The moon is bright, the night is glorious. It is my opinion that the apparition will not appear."

"I will take the precaution to put this in my pocket," I said, and I took up my revolver, which was loaded.

As I stepped out into the courtyard I found that the brilliant moonlight had lit up the north-west wall and the turrets; but the sharp black shadow of the south wall lay diagonally across the yard. Absolute stillness reigned, broken only by the croaking of thousands of frogs from the valley below. I sat down on a stone bench by the balustrade and tried to analyze my feelings. For a time the cheerfulness which I had seen so marked on De Castro's face seemed to have communicated itself to me; my late fears vanished, I was not even nervous, I found it difficult to concentrate my thoughts on the object which had brought me so far from England. My mind wandered back to London and to my work there. But by degrees, as the chill stole over me and the stillness of night began to embrace me, I found myself glancing ever and again at those countless windows and deep embrasures, while a queer, overpowering tension began to be felt, and against my own will a terror, strange and humiliating, overpowered me. I knew that it was stronger than I, and, fight against it as I would, I could not overcome it. The instinctive dread of the unknown that is at the bottom of the bravest man's courage was over me. Each moment it increased, and I felt that if the hideous face were to appear at one of the windows I would not be answerable for my self-control. Suddenly, as I sat motionless, my eyes riveted on the windows of the old castle, I felt, or fancied I felt, that I was not alone. It seemed to me that a shadow moved down in the courtyard and close to me. I looked again; it was coming towards me. It was with difficulty I could suppress the scream which almost rose to my lips. The next instant I was glad that I had not lost my self-control, when the slim, cold hand of Helen Sherwood touched mine.

"Come," she said, softly.

She took my hand and, without a word, led me across the courtyard.

"Look up," she said.

I did look up, and then my heart seemed to stop and every muscle in my body grew rigid as though from extreme cold. At one of the first-floor windows in the north-west tower, there in the moonlight leant the apparition itself: a black, solemn figure--its arms crossed on the sill--a large, round face of waxy whiteness, features immobile and fixed in a hideous, unwinking stare right across the courtyard.

My heart gave a stab of terror, then I remained absolutely rigid--I forgot the girl by my side in the wild beating of my pulse. It seemed to me that it must beat itself to death.

"Call my uncle," whispered Helen, and when I heard her voice I knew that the girl was more self-possessed than I was.

"Call him," she said again, "loudly--at once."

I shouted his name:--

"De Castro, De Castro; it is here!"

The figure vanished at my voice.

"Go," said Helen again. "Go; I will wait for you here. Follow it at once."

I rushed up the stairs towards the room where De Castro slept. I burst open his door. The room was empty. The next instant I heard his voice.

"I am here--here," he said. "Come at once---quick!"

In a moment I was at his side.

"This is the very room where it stood," I said.

I ran to the window and looked down. De Castro followed me. Helen had not moved. She was still gazing up-- the moonlight fell full on her white face.

"You saw it too?" gasped De Castro.

"Yes," I said, "and so did Helen. It stood by this window."

"I was awake," he said, "and heard your shout. I rushed to my window; I saw the specter distinctly, and followed it to this room. You swear you saw it? It was the face of the abbot."

My brain was working quickly, my courage was returning. The unfathomable terror of the night scene was leaving me. I took De Castro suddenly by both his arms and turned him round so that the moonlight should fall upon him.

"You and I are alone in this tower. Helen Sherwood is in the courtyard. There is not another living being in the whole castle. Now listen. There are only two possible explanations of what has just occurred. Either you are the specter, or it is supernatural."

"I?" he cried. "Are you mad?"

"I well might be," I answered, bitterly. "But of this I am certain: you must prove to me whether you are the apparition or not. I make this suggestion now in order to clear you from all possible blame; I make it that we may have absolute evidence that could not be upset before the most searching tribunal. Will you now strip before me?---yes, before you leave the room, and prove that you have no mask hidden anywhere on you. If you do this I shall be satisfied. Pardon my insistence, but in a case like the present there must be no loophole."

"Of course, I understand you," he said. "I will remove my clothes."

In five minutes he had undressed and dressed again. There was no treachery on his part. There was no mask nor any possible means of his simulating that face on his person.

"There is no suspicion about you," I said, almost with bitterness. "By heavens, I wish there were. The awfulness of this thing will drive me mad. Look at that girl standing by herself in the courtyard. I must return to her. Think of the courage of a woman who would stand there alone."

He made no answer. I saw that he was shivering.

"Why do you tremble?" I said, suddenly.

"Because of the nameless fear," he replied. "Remember I saw her father--I saw him with the terror on him--he ran along the battlements; he threw himself over--he died. He was dashed to pieces on the very spot where she is standing. Get her to come in, Druce."

"I will go and speak to her," I said.

I went back to the courtyard. I rejoined Helen, and in a few words told her what had occurred.

"You must come in now," I said. "You will catch your death of cold standing here."

She smiled a slow, enigmatic sort of smile.

"I have not given up the solution yet," she said, "nor do I mean to."

As she spoke she took her revolver from her belt, and I saw that she was strangely excited. Her manner showed intense excitement, but no fear.

"I suspect foul play," she said. "As I stood here and watched you and Uncle Petro talking to each other by that window I felt convinced--I am more than ever convinced----"

She broke off suddenly.

"Look!--oh, Heaven, look! What is that?"

She had scarcely uttered the words before the same face appeared at another window to the right. Helen gave a sharp cry, and the next instant she covered the awful face with her revolver and fired. A shrill scream rang out on the night air.

"It is human after all," said Helen; "I thought it was. Come."

She rushed up the winding stairs; I followed. The door of the room where we had seen the specter was open. We both dashed in. Beneath the window lay a dark huddled heap with the moonlight shining on it, and staring up with the same wide-open eyes was the face of the abbot. Just for a moment neither Helen nor I dared to approach it, but after a time we cautiously drew near the dark mass. The figure never moved. I ran forward and stretched out my hand. Closer and closer I bent until my hand touched the face. It was human flesh and was still warm.

"Helen," I said, turning to the girl, "go at once and find your uncle."

But I had scarcely uttered the words before Helen burst into a low, choking laugh--the most fearful laugh I had ever heard.

"Look, look!" she said.

For before our eyes the face tilted, foreshortened, and vanished. We were both gazing into the countenance of the man whom we knew as Petro de Castro. His face was bathed in blood and convulsed with pain. I lit the lantern, and as I once more approached I saw, lying on the ground by his side, something hairy which for an instant I did not recognize. The next moment I saw that it was--it explained everything. It was a wig. I bent still nearer, and the whole horrible deception became plain as daylight. for, painted upon the back of the man's perfectly bald head, painted with the most consummate skill, giving the startling illusion of depth and relief, and all the hideous expression that had terrified one man at least out of the world, was the face of the abbot. The wig had completely covered it, and so skillfully was it made that the keenest observer would never have suspected it was one, it being itself slightly bald in order to add to the deception.

There in that dim, bare room, in broken sentences, in a voice that failed as his life passed, De Castro faltered out the story of his sin.

"Yes," he said, "I have tried to deceive you, and Gonsalves aided me. I was mad to risk one more appearance. Bend nearer, both of you; I am dying. Listen.

"Upon this estate, not a league across the valley, I found six months ago alluvial gold in great quantities in the bed of the gully. In the 'Bibliotheca Publica' in Lisbon I had years before got accounts of mines worked by the Phoenicians, and was firmly persuaded that some of the gold still remained. I found it, and to get the full benefit of it I devised the ghastly scheme which you have just discovered. I knew that the castle was supposed to be haunted by the face of an old monk. Sherwood with all his peculiarities was superstitious. Very gradually I worked upon his fears, and then, when I thought the time ripe for my experiment, personated the apparition. It was I who flung him from the battlements with my own hand. I knew that the terms of the will would divert all suspicion from me, and had not your shot, Helen, been so true you would never have come here to live. Well, you have avenged your father and saved yourself at the same time. You will find in the safe in a corner of the banqueting-hall plans and maps of the exact spot where the gold is to be found. I could have worked there for years unsuspected. It is true that I should have lost ten thousand pounds, but I should have gained five times the amount. Between four and five months ago I went to see a special friend of mine in London. She is a woman who stands alone as one of the greatest criminals of her day. She promised at once to aid me, and she suggested, devised, and executed the whole scheme. She made the wig herself, with its strangely-bald appearance so deceptive to the ordinary eye, and she painted the awful face on my bald skull. When you searched me just now you suspected a mask, but I was safe from your detection. To remove or replace the wig was the work of an instant. The woman who had done all this was to share my spoils."

"Her name?" I cried.

"Sara, the Great, the Invincible," he murmured.

As he spoke the words he died.

IV. The Talk of the Town

THERE is such a thing as being haunted by an idea or by a personality. About this time Vandeleur and I began to have nightmares with regard to Mme. Sara. She visited us in our dreams, and in our waking dreams she was also our companion.

We suspected her unseen influence on all occasions. We dreaded to see her visible presence in the street, in the park, at the play – in short, wherever we went. This sort of thing was bad for both of us. It began to get on our nerves. It takes a great deal to get on the iron nerves of a man like Vandeleur; nevertheless, I began to think that they were seriously shaken when I received on a certain afternoon in late October, the following note:

"My Dear Druce: There are fresh developments in the grand hunt. Come and dine with me tomorrow evening to meet Prof. Piozzi. New problems are on foot."

The grand hunt could of course only mean one thing. What was she up to now? What in the name of fortune had Prof. Piozzi, the greatest and youngest scientist of the day, to do with Mme. Sara? But the chance of meeting him was a strong inducement for me to accept Vandeleur's invitation. He was our greatest experimental chemist. Six months ago his name had been on everyone's lips as the discoverer of a new artificial lighting agent which if commercially feasible, would take the place of all other means hitherto used.

Prof. Piozzi was not yet 36 years of age. He was an Italian by birth but spoke English as well as though it were his native tongue.

At the appointed hour I found Vandeleur standing by his hearth. A table in a distant recess was laid for dinner. He greeted me with a gleam of pleasure in his eyes.

"What is the new problem?" I asked. "It goes without saying that it has to do with Mme. Sara."

"I am glad you were able to come before Piozzi put in an appearance," was Vandeleur's grave answer.

He paused for an instant, and then he burst out in vehemence:

"I owe Sara a debt of gratitude. Hunting her as a recreation is as good as hunting a man-eating tiger. I am getting at her now by watching the movements of her victim."

"Who is the victim?" I interrupted.

"No less a person than Prof. Piozzi."

"Impossible." I answered.

Fact, all the same." He replied. "The professor, notwithstanding his genius is in many ways credulous, unsuspicious and easily imposed upon."

"Nevertheless, I fail to understand." I said.

"Have you ever heard of the subtle power of love?"

As Vendeleur spoke he stared hard at me, then burst into an uneasy laugh.

"The professor is in love." He said. "Madame's last move is truly prompted by genius. She has taken in exploiting one of the most extraordinary looking girls who have electrified society for mana a day. It isn't her mere beauty that draws everyone to Donna Maria; it is her peculiarity. She has all the ways of an unconscious siren, for never was anyone less self-conscious or more apparently indifferent to admiration."

"I have not heard of her." I said.

"Then you have allowed the talk of the town to slip past you, Druce," was Vandeleur's answer. "Donna Maria is the talk of the town. No one knows where she has sprung from; no one can confidently assert that this country or the other has had the honor of her nationality. She belongs to Mme. Sara; she accompanies her wherever she goes, and Prof. Piozzi is the victim."

"Are you sure?" I asked.

"Certain. He follows them like a shadow. Madame is keeping more or less in the background for the present. Donna Maria is the lure. We shall next hear of an engagement between our young friend and this girl, whose antecedents no one knows anything about. Madame has an object, of course. She means mischief."

It was my custom never to interrupt Vandeleur when he was explaining one of his theories, so I sat back in my chair and allowed him to proceed without comment on my part.

"At the present moment," he continued, "I happen to know that the professor has run to earth another of his amazing discoveries in the carbon compounds. No one but himself knows what it is as yet, not even his assistants. Next week he is going to explode the bombshell in the scientific world at a lecture at the Royal institution. Everyone will flock there on the tiptoe of expectation and curiosity. The thing is at present a dead secret, and the title of the lecture not even mentioned. He means to electrify the world. It is his little amusement to do this, as he did the ethylene light affair. The man is, of course, a phenomenon, a genius, probably the most brilliant of our times. He is absolutely unsuspicious and absolutely unworldly. I am not going to see him ruin himself if I can help it."

"I perceive that you are in earnest." I said: "but how are you to prevent a man who is his own master from adopting his own methods, even in the subtle cause of love? Supposing your young professor loves Donna Maria, how are you to stop him?"

"Time will prove how," he remarked; "but stop him I will."

The bell whirred and the next moment Prof. Piozzi entered. I looked at him with keen interest. From his photographs, reproduced freely in the illustrated papers, I had expected to see a young and good-looking man, with a keen, intelligent face; but I was scarcely prepared for his juvenile appearance. He was tall in figure, well made, somewhat slender; his hair was of a fair flaxen shade; his eyes were wide open and of a clear blue. He had a massive forehead, dark eyebrows and a clean shaven face. His whole appearance was that of an ordinary, good-looking man, everyday sort of young man, and I examined his features with extreme curiosity, endearing to detect anywhere a sign of genius. I could not do so. The professor's whole appearance was everyday; not a doubt of it. He was well dressed and had an easy, courteous manner, and upon a finger of his left hand there gleamed a ring, a royal gift from the king of his native land.

We sat down to dinner, and the conversation was light, pleasant and sufficiently witty to cause the moments to fly. No one knew better than Vandeleur how to make a man feel at home in his own house and I could see that Piozzi was enjoying himself in a boyish way.

It was not until the meal was nearly over that the professor caused us both to start, and listen, with extreme attention. He began to talk of Mme. Sara. He spoke of her with enthusiasm. She was the cleverest woman in London and, with one exception, the most beautiful. Her scientific accomplishments were marvelous. He considered himself extremely lucky to have made her acquaintance.

"The sort of knowledge you allude to," replied Vandeleur, in a very grave tone, "that scientific knowledge which Madame possesses, and which is not a smattering, but a real thing, makes a woman at times ------ dangerous."

"I do not follow you." Replied the professor, knitting his brows. "Madame is the reverse of dangerous; she would help a fellow at a pinch. She is as good as she is beautiful."

Vandeleur made no reply. I was about to speak, but I saw by his manner that he would rather turn the conversation.

Once more we chatted on less exciting topics and it was not until the servants had withdrawn that Vandeleur proceeded to unfold the real business of the evening.

"So you are going to astonish us all next week professor, at the Royal Institution? Is it true that you, and you alone, possess the key of the discourse that you are to give us?"

"Quite true." He replied with a smile. "I cannot help having the dramatic instincts of my race. I love an artistic effect, and I think I can guarantee you English chemists a little thrill on Saturday. My paper was ready a month ago, and since completing it I have been having a pleasant time. Until a month ago your London was more or less a closed book to me. Now, Mme. Sara and her young companion, Donna Maria, have been taking me round. I have enjoyed myself, not a doubt of it."

He leaned back in his chair and smiled.

"That woman does plan things in a most delightful manner." He continued, "and whether she entertains in her own wonderful reception rooms at the back of her shop in the Strand, or whether I meet her at the houses of mutual friends, or at the play, or the opera, she is always bright, vivacious, charming. Donna Maria, of course, adds her share to the delights. Yes, it is all happiness," continued the young professor, rubbing his hands together in a boyish manner. "You English," he added, fixing his bright blue eye on Vandeleur's saturnine face, "are so dull---I might add--- *triste*. And yet," he added quickly, "you have your charm. Oh, undoubtedly yes. Your sincerity is so marvelous. I ought to add — refreshing. One can rely on it. But Madame has also the sincere air, and yet to her are given the brightness and vivacity which come from living under bluer skies than yours."

The professor's face was flushed; he looked from Vandeleur to me with eagerness. Vandeleur drew his chair a trifle closer. Then, without warning, as though he could not help himself, he sprang to his feet.

"Prof. Piozzi," He said, "you have given our nation, perhaps unwittingly, a rare and valuable tribute. You have just spoken of our sincerity. I trust that we are sincere, and I trust also that so long as England remains England, an Englishman's word will be his bond. The best inheritance an Englishman can receive from his forefathers is the power on all occasions to speak the truth. You are my guest tonight. I have the greatest respect for you; I admire your genius as I never thought to admire the genius of any man. It is most painful to me to have to say a word that may seem discourteous to you, an honored guest, but my heritage as an Englishman forces me to speak the truth. You know what I am--- an official criminal agent of the police. I will be quite candid with you. My invitation to you tonight was not purely the disinterested one of enjoying the honor of your company, but also to give you a warning with regard to Mme. Sara and the young girl who accompanies her into society. They are both dangerous. I speak with knowledge. It is true that the girl herself is in all probability only the tool; but the woman---- --! Professor, I have met that woman before; so has my friend Druce. Our acquaintance with her has not been agreeable. May I proceed?"

The profesor's face had now turned almost crimson; his blue eyes were staring from his head; he kept clenching and unclenching his right hand as though he could scarcely contain himself. Vandeleur's words, however, seemed to force him into an attitude of attention. He listened as though mesmerized.

My friend then proceeded to give a vivid sketch of some of the episodes which had fallen to our share in the life of Mme. Sara. He spoke slowly, with great emphasis and precision. He stated his case as though he were addressing a jury in a court of justice, scoring point after point with brevity and brilliance. When at last he ceased to speak the professor was silent for half a minute, then he rose with a jerk to his feet. He was trembling, and his eyes flashed fire.

"Mr. Vandeleur," he said, "we are acquaintances of only a year's standing; in that time we have had some pleasant interviews. Your business is not an attractive one, even when confined to its official precincts; but to introduce it into private affairs is not to be tolerated. You exceed the limits of propriety in dictating to me as to the choice of the list of my friends. Please understand that from that list I erase your name."

He bowed stiffly, and walking across the room took up his hat and coat and slammed the door behind him.

I glanced at Vandeleur in amazement. His eyes met mine.

"The man must have his fling." he said. "I did what I did for the best, and am not sorry. He is in love with the mysterious girl, who has been brought to England, doubtless for the express purpose of working his ruin.. We must find out all we can about her as quickly as possible. Poor young professor. I should like to save him, and I will too, if in the power of man. His powers of research must not be lost to the glories of the scientific world."

"You must admit, Vandeleur," I said, "that you were a trifle harsh in your dealings with him. Granted that he is in love with Donna Maria, can you expect him to take your warning tamely?"

Vandeleur was silent for a minute.

"I do not believe my sever words will do any harm in the long run," he said, "The man is a foreigner; he has not an Englishman's knack of keeping his temper under control. He will cool down presently and what I have said will return to him. They will come to him when he is talking to Donna Maria; when Mme. Sara is throwing her spells over him. Yes, I am not sorry I have spoken."

"What do you suppose Madame is after?" I interrupted. "What can be her motive?" It is not money, for the man is not well off, is he?"

"Not a thousand a year. Bah! And, he might be a millionaire if he would only use his ideas commercially. It is the old story—one man finds the brains and a hundred others profit by them. He is a walking test-tube and doesn't care a sou who profits by his inventions."

"Then you think she is picking his brains?"

"Of course, and she will pick a plum too, bang it off in England, scoop a million, and we have lost her."

"Good for society if we do lose her." I could not help remarking.

"By no means good for me," replied the detective. "I have staked my reputation on bringing this woman to book. She shall not escape."

Vandeleur and I sat and talked for some time longer, then I left him and returned to my own rooms. I sat up a long time busy over several matters; but when I retired to rest it was not only to dream of Mme. Sara, but of the fascinating young Donna Marta and the boyish-looking professor.

I dined with Vandeleur on Wednesday evening, and little guessed then how soon events would hurry to a remarkable issue, in which I was to play a somewhat important part.

It is my custom to lunch at the Ship and Turtle, an hour that I always enjoy in the midst of my day's work, for I meet many old friends there and our meal, as a rule, is a merry one. One of my constant companions on these occasions is a man of the name of Samuel Pollak, the senior partner in the firm of Pollack & Harman, patent agents. Bishopgate Street. Pollak is one of those breezy, good-natured individuals who make a pleasant impression wherever they go. He is stout of build and somewhat round of face, an excellent man of business and a firm friend. I have liked him for years and am always glad when he occupies the same table with me at lunch.

On the Friday following Vandeleur's dinner, Pollak and I met as usual. I noticed on his entrance into the lunch room a particularly merry and pleased expression on his face. He sat down and ordered a quart of the most expensive brand of champagne. He insisted on my joining him in a bumper of the frothy wine, and after drinking his health I could not help exclaiming:

"You seem pretty jolly this morning, Pollak. A successful flutter in khakis?"

"Ha, ha, ha!" was the answer. "Better than a flutter my boy. Certainties, nowadays are what I am thinking of, and I have just bagged one, and a fat one."

"Capital. Tell me all about it." I answered. "What is the yarn, Pollak?"

He gave me a somewhat vague smile, which seemed to me to mingle a sort of contempt with amusement, and said, impressively.

"A roaring commission, the biggest that has been in the market for the last ten years. Patent rights for every country on earth, and a hundred shares allotted gratis when the thing is floated. I tell you, Druce, "he added, raising his voice, "If it comes off I retire with as near fifteen thousand dollars a year as I want."

"You were born under a lucky star, there's no doubt of that." I answered, somewhat sharply, for Pollak's manner had never impressed me less favorably than it did this morning. He was evidently almost beside himself with excitement.

"I congratulate you, of course." I said, after a moment. "Ask me to the house-warming of your castle in Scotland whenever that event comes off. But can't you give me a hint with regard to this magnificent affair? I am, as you know, a struggling pauper, and I should like to have a share of the pickings if there are any at your disposal to give away."

"My lips are sealed." He answered at once. "I am sorry for there is no one I should like better to help. But I think I am justified in telling you this — the city will hum when the news is out. It is immense. It is colossal. It is paralyzing."

"You excite my curiosity to a remarkable extent." I could not help saying. "Curiosity has a great deal to do with my trade as you know."

He finished his glass of champagne and set it down. His eyes, as he fixed them on me, were full of laughter. I almost wondered whether he was amusing himself at my expense, but no, his next words were sane enough.

"There is another little matter I can inform you about, Druce, without breaking any confidence. I happen to know that the fortunate patentee is a friend of yours."

"A friend of mine?" I exclaimed. "An acquaintance, perhaps. I haven't three friends in the world."

"A great friend — an admirer, too," he went on.

"An admirer!" I repeated, staring across at him. "A devoted admirer! Who is he? Come out with it Pollak; don't keep me on tenterhooks."

"Think over your list of admirers." He cried, tantalizingly.

"I will hazard a guess, then! But he isn't an admirer. Vandeleur," I cried.

"Ha, ha!" he roared. "Better and better. She admires him too, I believe."

"She!"

A strange thought seized me. I felt the high spirits which Pollak had infected me with depart as in a flash. I knew that in spite of every effort my face had altered in expression. Pollak gazed at me an said, in a tone of triumph:

"I see that you guess. That cat is out of the bag."

He chuckled.

"Isn't it superb?" he added.

"Mme. Sara!" I ejaculated, when I could find words.

He burst into a fresh roar of delight.

"There's no harm in your knowing that much," he said. "but what's up? You look queer."

The change in my demeanor must have astonished him. I sat almost motionless, staring into his face.

"Nothing." I answered, speaking as quietly as I could. "The admiration you have remarked upon is reciprocal. I am glad that she has done so well."

"She is particularly pleased," continued Pollak, "on account of her young protégé, the lovely Donna Marta. The young lady in question is to make a very good match—in a certain sense a brilliant one; and Madame wants to give her a wedding portion. Ah! There are few women so kind, so great, as Mme. Sara. She has the wisdom of the ancients, and some of their secrets, too."

I made no reply. The usual thing had happened so far as my good-natured friend was concerned. He was dazzled by the beauty of his client, and had given himself away, a ready victim to her fascinations.

"I see," he added, "that you are also under her spells. Who wouldn't yield to the power of those eyes? The young lady, Donna Marta is all very well, but give me Madame herself."

With these words he left me. Never was there a more prosperous or happier looking man. Little did he guess the thoughts that were surging in my brain.

Without returning to my place of business I took a hansom and drove to Vandeleur's office. My heart was full of nameless fear. Pollack had let out a great deal more than he had any intention of doing. So Donna Marta was engaged. Engaged to whom? Surely not to the poor, infatuated young professor? Pollak had said that in some respects the proposed match was a brilliant one. That might be a fitting description of a marriage with the young professor, whose fame was attracting the attention of the greatest scientists in Europe. He was poor, certainly—but then he held a secret. That secret might mean anything—it might even revolutionize the world.

Did Madame mean by this subtle trap to lure it from him? It was more than probable. It would explain Pollak's excitement and his attitude. In fact, the scheme was worthy of her colossal brain.

As I entered Vandeleur's room I was surprised to see him pacing up and down with his coat off, his brows knitted in anxious thought. He was evidently in the thick of a problem, and one of no ordinary magnitude. On the table lay a number of beakers, retorts and test tubes.

"Sit down," he said roughly, "Glad you came. See this?"

He held up a glass tube containing what appeared to be milk.

"Listen," he said. "You will see that my fears were justified with regard to Piozzi. Poor fellow, he is in the toils, if ever a man was. A hurried messenger came from his place to fetch me this morning. I guessed by his face that something serious had happened, and I went to Duke Street at once. I found the professor in his bed-room, half dressed on his bed, cold, gasping, livid. He had breakfasted half an hour before. He murmured apologies for his treatment of me, but I cut him short and went straight to the case. I made a full investigation, and came to the conclusion that it is a case of poisoning, the agent used being in all probability cocaine or some allied alkaloid. By the aid of nitrate of amyl capsules I pulled him round, but was literally only just in time. When I entered the room it was touch and go with the poor fellow. I believe if he had not had immediate assistance he would have been dead in a few minutes. I saved his life. Now, Druce, we have to face a fact. There has been a deliberate attempt at murder on the part of someone. I have baffled the murderer in the moment of victory."

"Who would attempt his life?" I cried.

"Need you ask?" he answered gravely.

Our eyes met. We were both silent.

"When I was with him this morning he was too bad for me to get any particulars whatever from him, so I know nothing of the motive or details; but I have discovered by means of a careful analysis that there has been introduced into the milk with which he was supplied some poisonous alkaloid of the erythroxiyon group. Feeling pretty certain that the poison was conveyed through the food, I took away a portion of his breakfast—in particular I took some of the milk which stood in a jug on his breakfast table. And, here I have the result. I am going back there at once and you had better come along."

Vandeleur had poured out his words in such a torrent of excitement that he had not noticed how unusual it was for me to visit him at this early hour in the afternoon. Now, however, it seemed to strike him, and he said abruptly:

"You look strange yourself. Surely you haven't come here on purpose? You can't possibly have heard of this thing yet?"

"No." I answered. "I have heard nothing. I have come on my own account, and on a pretty big matter, too. And, what is more, it relates to our young professor, unless I am much mistaken. I will tell you what I have to tell in the cab, Vandeleur, it will save time."

A hansom was summoned and we were soon on our way to Duke Street. As we drove I told Vandeleur in a few words what had occurred between Pollak and myself. He listened with the intentness which always characterized him. He made not a single remark.

126

As we were entering the house, however, he turned to me and said, with brevity;

"It is clear that she has tapped him. We must get from him what she knows. This may be a matter of millions."

On arriving at Piozzi's flat in Duke Street we were at once shown into his bed-room by his man servant. Stretched upon the outside of the bed was the young professor, wrapped in a loose dressing gown. His face was ghastly pale, and there was a blue tinge observable round his mouth and under his eyes. He raised himself languidly as we entered.

"Better. I see. Capital!" said Vandeleur, in a cheerful tone.

A very slight color came into the young man's face. He glanced at me almost in bewilderment.

"You know my friend, Druce," said Vandeleur. "He is with me in this case, and has just brought me important information. Lie down again, professor."

As he spoke he sat on the edge of the bed and laid his hand on the young man's arm.

"I am sorry to have to tell you, Mr. Piozzi, that this is a very serious case. A rapid qualitative analysis of what you took for breakfast has shown me that the mild which was supplied for your use has been poisoned. What the poison is I cannot say. It is very like cocaine in its reactions."

The sick man shuddered and an expression of horror and amazement crossed his face.

"Who would want to take my life?" he said. "Poisoned milk! I confess I do not understand. The thing must have been accidental," he continued feverishly, fixing his puzzled eyes on Vandeleur.

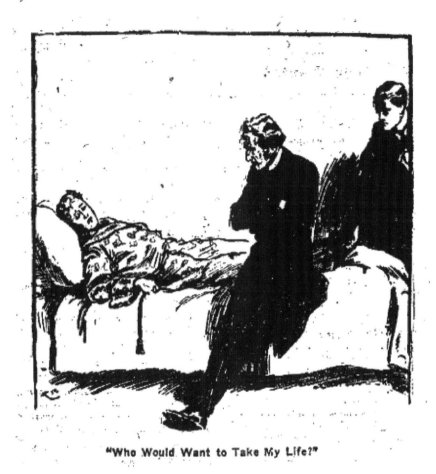

"Who Would Want to Take My Life?"

Vandeleur shook his head.

"There was no accident in this matter." He said with emphasis. "It was design. Deadly too. You would not have been alive now if I had not come to you in the nick of time. It is our duty professor, to go carefully into every circumstance in order to insure you against a farther attempt on your life."

"But I do no one harm." He answered irritably. "Who could wish to take my life from me? It is impossible. You are laboring under a wrong impression."

"We will let the motive rest for the present." replied Vandeleur. "That the attempt was made is certain. Our present object is to discover how the poison got into the mild. That is the question that must be answered and before Druce and I leave this room. Who supplies you with the milk Prof. Piozzi?"

Piozzi replied by a languid motion towards the bell.

"My man will tell you." he said. "I know nothing more about the matter."

The servant was summoned and his information was brief and to the point. The professor's milk was supplied by the same milkman who supplied all the other members of the mansion.

"It is brought early in the morning sir." said the man, "and left outside the door of each flat. The housekeeper opens the house door for the purpose. I take it in myself the first thing on rising."

"And the can remains outside your door with the house door open until you take it in?" said Vandeleur.

"Yes sir, of course."

"Thank you." said Vandeleur. "That will do."

The man left the room.

"You see professor," remarked my friend after the door had closed upon the servant, "how simple the matter is. Anyone could drop poison into the milk—that is, of course,

129

what somebody did. These modern arrangements don't take crime into account when criminal means business."

The professor lay still, evidently thinking deeply. I noticed then, for the first time, that a look of age had crept over his face. It improved him, giving stability and power to features too juvenile for the mass of knowledge which that keen brain contained. His eyes were full of trouble; it was evident that is meditations were the reverse of satisfactory.

"I am the last man to pretend not to see when a self-evident fact stares me in the face." he said at last. "There has been an attempt made to poison me. But by whom? Can you tell me that, Mr. Vandeleur?"

"I could give you a very shrewd guess." replied Vandeleur; "but were I to name my suspicions you would be offended."

"Forgive me for my exhibition of rage the other night." He answered quite humbly. "Speak your mind—I shall respect you whatever you say."

"In my mind's eye, "said Vandeleur slowly, "I see a woman who has before attempted the life of those whom she was pleased to call her friends."

The professor started to his feet. Notwithstanding his vehement assertion that he would not give way to his emotions, he was trembling all over.

"You cannot mean Mme. Sara—you will change your mind—I have something to confide. Between now and last Wednesday I have been affianced to Donna Maria. Yes, we are to marry and soon. Madame is beside herself with bliss and Donna Maria herself—Ah, I have no words to speak what my feelings are with regard to her. Madame of all people would be the last to murder me." he added wildly, "for she loves Donna Maria."

"I am deeply sorry, professor, notwithstanding your words and the very important statement you have just made with regard to the young lady who lives with Mme. Sara to have to adhere to my opinion that there is a very deep-laid plot on foot and that it menaces your life. I still believe that Madame notwithstanding your word is head and center of that plot. Take my statement for what it is worth. It is. I can assure you the only thing that I can say. And now I must ask you a few questions and you must have patience with me, great patience, while you reply to them. I beg of you to tell me the truth absolutely and frankly."

"I will" answered the young man. "You move me strangely. I cannot help believing in you, although I hate myself for allowing one suspicious thought to fall on her."

Vandeleur rose.

"Tell me, Mr. Piozzi," he said quietly, "have you ever communicated to Mme. Sara the nature of your chemical discoveries?"

"Never."

"Has she ever been here?"

"Oh yes, many times. Last week she and Donna Maria were both here. I had a little reception for them. We enjoyed ourselves; she was delightful."

"You have several rooms in this flat, have you not, professor?"

"Three reception rooms" he answered rather wearily.

"And you and Donna Maria were perhaps alone in one of those rooms while Mme. Sara amused herself in another? Is that so?"

"It is." he answered, reddening. "Madame and Donna Maria remained after my other guests had gone. Madame went into my study. She said she would sit by the fire and rest."

"Do you leave your notes locked up or lying about?"

"Always locked up. It is true the notes for my coming lecture were on that occasion on my desk."

"Ah," Interrupted Vandeleur.

"No ordinary person could make anything of them." he continued; "and even," he added, "if Madame could have read them it surely would not greatly matter that she should know my grand secret before the rest of the world."

"Piozzi." said Vandeleur very gravely, "I must make another request of you. Whether Madame knows your secret or not I must know it at once. Don't hesitate, professor; your life hangs in the balance. You must tell me that with which you mean to electrify the Royal Institute tomorrow week. Now. Now at once."

The professor looked astonished, but Vandeleur was firm.

"I must know it." he said. "I hold myself responsible for your life. Druce," he added, turning to me, "perhaps you can get the professor to see the necessity of what I ask. Will you tell him that story which you related to me in the cab?"

I did so without a moment's delay. My words were as brief as I could make them. I told him about my interview with Pollak, his excitement, his revelation of the fact that the patentee whose patent was to be secured in all countries all over the world was no less a person than Mme. Sara herself. In short, to my infinite delight, I managed to convey my suspicions to his mind. His whole attitude altered; he became excited, almost beside himself. His nervousness gave place to unexpected strength. He started to his feet and began to pace the room.

"Heavens!" he exclaimed more than once. "If indeed I have been befooled—made a dupe of—but not, it cannot be. Still, if it is, I will revenge myself on Madame to the last drop of my blood."

"For the present you must only confide in me." said Vandeleur, laying a restraining hand on the young man's arm. "And now for your secret—it is safe with Druce and myself; we must know it."

Piozzi calmed down as suddenly as he had given way to rage. He seated himself on a sofa and began in a quiet voice. "What I have to say is simply this."

Then in terse language he poured out for Vandeleur's benefit an account of some process, saturated with formulae, equations and symbols, absolutely beyond my comprehension.

Vandeleur sat and listened intently. Now and then he put a question, which was immediately answered. At last Piozzi had come to the end of his narrative.

"That is it." he said, "the whole thing in a nutshell."

"Upon my word." said Vandeleur. "It is very ingenious and plausible, and may turn out of immense benefit to the world, but at the present juncture I cannot see money in it and money is what Madame wants and means to have. To

133

be frank with you professor, I see no earthly reason in her wanting to patent what you have just told me. But is there nothing else? Are you certain?"

"Absolutely nothing." Was his response.

"Well," said Vandeleur, "I am puzzled. I own it. I must think matters over."

He was interrupted by a loud exclamation from the young man.

"You are wrong after all, Mr. Vandeleur," he cried. "Madame means to patent something else. Why should she not have a great idea in her head quite apart from me and mine? Ah, this relieves me — it makes me happy. True, someone has tried to murder me, but it is not Madame — it is not the lady whom Donna Maria loves."

His eyes blazed with delight. He laughed in feverish excitement.

After soothing him as best we could and trying to get a half promise that he would not see either Madame or the young lady until we met again, we left him.

As we were walking from the house Vandeleur turned to me and said:

"I have been invited to a reception tonight at the house of our mutual friends the Lauderdales. I understand that both Madame and the young lady are to be present. Would you like to come with me? I am allowed to bring a friend."

I eagerly assented. We arranged when and where to meet and were about to part when he suddenly exclaimed:

"This is a difficult problem. I shall have no rest until I have solved it. Piozzi's discovery is ingenious and clever but at present it is unworkable. I do not see daylight, but no loophole is to be despised that may give me what I want. Between now and our meeting this evening I will try to have an interview with Pollak. Give me his address."

I did so and we parted.

We met again at a late hour that evening at the Lauderdales beautiful house in Portland place. Wit and beauty were to be found in the gay throng, also wisdom and a fair sprinkling of some of the most brilliant brains in London. Men of note came face to face with one in every direction; but both Vandeleur and I were seeking one face and one alone.

We found her at last surrounded by a throng of admirers. Madame was looking her most brilliant and I might add, her youngest self. She was dressed in dazzling white and silver and whenever she moved, light seemed to be reflected at every point. The brilliance of her golden hair was the only distinct color about her. By her side stood Donna Maria, a tall, pale girl, almost too slender for absolute beauty. Her grace, however, was undeniable and, although I have seen more lovely faces, this one had a singular power of attraction. When I looked at her once I wanted to look again, and when she slowly raised her luminous eyes and fixed them on my face I owned to a thrill of distinct gratification. I began to understand the possibility of Piozzi's giving himself up absolutely to her charms.

Her presence here tonight, in conjunction with Mme. Sara produced an effect which was as astonishing as it was rare. Each acted as a perfect foil to the other. Each seemed to bring out the pure fascination of her companion.

Donna Maria glanced at me again: then I saw her bend towards Mme. Sara and whisper something in her ear. A moment later, to my amusement, the great lady and the slender girl were by my side.

"Mr. Druce, this is an unexpected pleasure. May I introduce you to my young cousin, Donna Maria? Is your friend Mr. Vandeleur also here tonight?"

"He is, I will find him." I replied.

I darted away, returning in a moment with Vandeleur. He and madame moved a few paces away and began to chat in pleasant tones, just as though they were the best friends in the world.

Meanwhile Donna Maria lingered near me. I began to talk on indifferent subjects, but she interrupted me abruptly.

"You are a friend of Prof. Piozzi's?" she said in a tentative voice. "Is he not present tonight?"

"No," I replied. It occurred to me that I would test her. "The professor cannot be present and I am sorry to have to give a grave reason for his absence, for doubtless Lady Lauderdale expected him to grace her reception."

"She did, he was to be one of the guests." she replied, bending her stately head, with its mass of blue-black hair.

"He is ill," I continued, raising my own eyes now and fixing them on her face.

She gazed at me without alarm and without confusion. Not the most remote emotion did she show, and yet she was engaged to the man.

"He was at death's door." I went on almost savagely, "but he is better. For the present he is safe."

"I am sorry to hear of his illness," she answered them softly. "I will-acquaint Madame. She also will be grieved."

"I am Sorry to Hear of His Illness," She Said.

The girl turned and gilded away from me. I watched her as she went. The brief moment when she fascinated me had come to an end with that callous glance. But who was she? What did it all mean?

In the course of the evening Donna Maria came up to my side.

"Mr. Druce" she said abruptly, "you are Prof. Piozzi's friend?"

"Certainly," I answered.

"Will you warn him from yourself — not from me — not on any account from me — to keep in the open Saturday week? You must make the best of my words for I cannot explain them. Tell the professor whatever he does to keep in the open."

"Donna Maria!" called Mme. Sara's voice.

The girl sprang away. Her face was like death; but as Mme. Sara's eyes met hers I noticed a wave of crimson dye on her face and neck.

On my way home I told Vandeleur of the strange words used by Donna Maria. He shrugged his shoulders.

"It is my firm opinion," he said, "that the unfortunate girl moves and speaks in a state of trance. Madame has mesmerized her. I have not a doubt of it."

"You may be right." I said eagerly. "And the state of trance may have been removed when she said those words to me. That would make a possible solution. But what can she mean by asking the professor to keep in the open?"

"The girl evidently warns us against Mme. Sara," he said briefly, "and circumstances, all circumstances, seem to point to the same deadly danger. Where Madame goes death walks abroad. What is to be done? But there, Druce," he added with petulance, "the professor's life is not my affair. I must sleep or I shall lose my senses. Good night, good night."

The next few days passed without any special occurrences of interest. At last the day dawned which was to see Prof. Piozzi in the moment of his glory. I had a line from Vandeleur by the first post, telling me that he had secured tickets for himself and for me for the lecture at the Royal Institution that night. Soon afterward I found myself at Vandeleur's house. His servant opened the door and with a look of relief asked me to up to the sitting room without delay. I was expected, then, or at least I was wished for.

The first person I saw when I entered the room was my old friend, Samuel Pollack, and gazing round in some astonishment I also perceived the young professor, buried in the depths of an arm chair, his face ghastly and his arm in a sling.

"Ah, Druce," said Vandeleur,"you are heartily welcome. You have come in the nick of time. I was just about to clear up this extraordinary affair in the presence of Mr. Pollack and the professor. Your advent on the scene makes my audience complete. Now, gentlemen, pray listen. The patent, Mr. Pollak, which you are negotiating for Mme. Sara is, as you imagine, a secret. I don't ask you to tell me what it is, for I propose to tell you. But, first, are your operations for securing patent rights complete?"

"I regret to say they are not, sir." replied Pollak.

"I thought as much and may add that I hoped as much. Now listen. The key to the specification of the patents is nothing more or less than the astounding discovery of the chemical synthesis of albuminoids, in other words, a means of manufacturing artificial foods in a manner which has long

139

been sought by scientific men, but which has so far eluded their researches."

An exclamation of astonishment broke from Pollak, telling us that Vandeleur's guess was correct.

"The other day when you spoke to me professor," continued Vandeleur, fixing his eyes on the face of the younger man, "interesting as I thought your discovery, I could not apply it to commercial purposes, nor see why it was so necessary to secure patent rights for its protection. I felt certain, however, that there was such a solution, and it came to me in the small hours this morning. You did not grasp the deduction from your most interesting discovery. I take it to my credit that I have done so and beyond doubt Madame, whether she be your friend or foe, perceived the huge financial benefit which would accrue to those who could hold patent rights. It goes without saying that she read your notes and at a glance saw what you have not grasped at all, and what I have taken days to discover. The attempt on your life is now explained, as is also the queer cab accident in Regent street which you have just met with. Madame's object is either to murder you or to incapacitate you from giving your lecture tonight. She knows, of course, that when once you publicly proclaim your discovery a clever brain on the watch may deduce the financial value of it. Thus she sees the possibility of being forestalled or rivaled for Mr. Pollak has just stated that the patent rights are not yet secured. Madame has therefore determined that your lecture shall not take place nor your idea be given to the world until she has secured herself by patent rights beyond dispute. I shall take care to guard you, professor, until you appear before the Royal society at 8 o'clock tonight. And, I conclude, Mr Pollak, that you, knowing at last the true facts of the case, will at once cancel all negotiations with Mme. Sara. I presume, sir," he added, bowing to Piozzi, "that you will like him to negotiate the business in your name? A cursory inspection of it must mean an enormous fortune for you, far beyond doubt the chemical synthesis of ailments would prove the solution of many of the difficulties that now present themselves to the human race."

The professor sat quite silent for a minute or two, then he rose and said, slowly:

"I follow you, Mr. Vandeleur, and I see that your deduction is the right one as regards the financial importance of my discovery. How I did not see it sooner myself puzzles me. As to Mme. Sara, I would rather not mention her name at present."

"Well," said Vandeleur. "If Prof. Piozzi declines to talk of Mme. Sara, neither will I mention her name. We shall soon know the best or the worst."

The rest of the day passed without adventure. The dinner at Vandeleur's turned out somewhat dull. We were none of us in good spirits, and, without owning it, we were all anxious. As to the professor, he scarcely spoke a word and hardly touched his food.

About 8:10 o'clock we found ourselves at the Royal Institution. Several leading scientists were there to welcome the distinguished lecturer. I peeped from behind ingot the hall. It was packed from front to back. The platform was tastefully decorated with palms, one of peculiar grace and size drooped its finger-like fronts over the table at which Piozzi was to stand. As I saw it I heard as distinctly as thought the words were again being spoken:

"Tell him whatever he does to keep in the open. Tell him — from yourself."

I had not done so. A momentary impulse seized me. I would go to Piozzi and ask him to have his table and chair moved to the center of the platform. Then I reflected that such a proceeding would cause amazement and that the professor would probably refuse to comply. Again I looked into the hall, and now I gave a very visible start, for in the front row, in brilliant evening dress, sat Mme. Sara and her young cousin. Donna Maria's face, usually so pale, was now relieved by a crimson glow on each cheek. This unusual color brought out her beauty to a dazzling degree. I notice further that her eyes had a filmy expression in them. I remembered Vandeleur's words. Beyond a doubt Madame had mesmerized her victim. As to what it all meant, I will own that my own brain was in a whirl.

A few minutes passed and then amid a thunder of applause, Piozzi, pale as ivory, stepped on to the platform and walked straight to the table over which hung the graceful palm.

After a few words in which the young professor was introduced by the president of the evening, the lecture about which so much curiosity had been felt began. Vandeleur and I stood side by side near one of the entrance doors. From where we stood we could see Piozzi well. Vandeleur's face was rigid as steel.

A quarter of an hour passed, and sentence by sentence, word by word, the young man led up to his crucial point — his great announcement.

"Look!" whispered Vandeleur grasping my wrist. "What in the world is the matter with him?"

The professor was still speaking, but his words came in thick and indistinct sentences. Suddenly he took hold of the table with both hands to sway to and fro. The next moment he ceased speaking, reeled, made a lunge forward and, with a loud crash, fell senseless upon the floor. The scene of consternation was indescribable. Vandeleur and I both sprang forward. The unconscious man was taken into one of the ante-rooms, and by the immediate application of restoratives and a great draft of fresh air, caused by the open windows, he came gradually to himself. But that he was still very ill was evident; his brain was confused: he could scarcely speak except in gasps. A doctor who was present offered to see him to his house. We carried him to the first cab we could find. I whispered in his ear that I would call upon him later in the evening and then I returned to the hall.

He Reeled and Made a Lunge Forward.

Vandeleur was waiting for me. I felt his grip on my arm.

"Come right up onto the platform." he said.

The excitement in his voice was only exceeded by the look on his face. Most of the crowd had dispersed, knowing well that there would be no further lecture that night, but a few people still lingered on the scene. I looked in vain for Mme. Sara and Donna Maria; they were neither of them visible.

"You see this." said Vandeleur, pointing to the great palm that towered over the table at which Piozzi stood. "And you see this." he repeated, seizing one of the branches and shaking it.

The long, tapering green leaves rattled together with an odd, metallic sound.

"Look here!" said Vandeleur, and he pointed to the fine tips of one of the leaves. "This plant never grew. It is made — It is an artificial imitation of the most surprising skill and workmanship. The pot in which it stands has certainly earth at the top," — he swept away a handful — "but there below is a receptacle which is generating carbon monoxide gas."

He bent and broke one of the branches.

"Hollow, you see. Those are the tubes to convey the gas to the leaves at the extremity of each of which is an orifice. Prof. Piozzi was standing beneath a veritable shower bath of that gas, which is odorless and colorless and brings insensibility and death. It overwhelmed him, as you saw, and it was impossible for him to finish his lecture. Only one human being could have planned and executed such a contrivance. If we can trace it to her, she spends the night in Bow Street."

144

Our movements were rapid. The plant was taken to Vandeleur's house. The florist who had supplied the decorations was interviewed. He expressed himself astounded. He denied all complicity — the palm was certainly none of his; he could not tell how it had got into the hall. He had come himself to see if the decorations were carried out according to his instructions and had noticed the palm and remarked on its grace. Someone had said that a lady had brought it, but he really knew nothing definite about it.

Notwithstanding all our inquiries, neither did we ever find out how that palm got mixed up with the others. There was however, one satisfaction — the plot, on which so much hung, had failed. Madame was not successful. Prof. Piozzi, his eyes opened at last with regard to this woman, took out his patent without an hour of unnecessary delay.

V. The Bloodstone

ON a certain bright spring morning Violet Sale married Sir John Bouverie, and six months later, when autumn was fast developing into a somewhat rigorous winter, I received an invitation to spend a week or fortnight at their beautiful place, Greylands, in the neighborhood of Potters Bar. Violet at the time of her marriage was only 19 years of age. She and her brother Hubert were my special friends. They were by many years my juniors, but their mother at her death had asked me to show them friendship and to advise them in any troubles that might arise in circumstances of their lives. They were both charming young people, and having been left complete control of quite a large property were in a somewhat exceptional position. Hubert was remarkably handsome and Violet had the freshness and charm of a true English girl.

On the evening before my visit to Greylands, Vandeleur came to seem me. He looked restless and ill at ease.

"So you are going to spend a fortnight at the Bouveries?" he said.

146

"Yes." I replied. "I look forward with giant pleasure to the visit. Violet being such an old friend of mine."

"It is a curious fact," said Vandeleur, "that Bouverie is an old friend of mine. Did I mention to you that I spent a week with them both in Scotland two months ago? I had then the privilege of prescribing for Lady Bouverie."

"Indeed!" I answered in some amazement. "I did not know that you gave your medical services except to your own division of police."

He laughed.

"My-dear fellow, what is a doctor worth if he doesn't on all occasions and under every circumstance practice when required the healing art? Lady Bouverie was in a very low condition; her nerves were out of order – in fact, I never saw anyone such a complete wreck. I prescribed some heroic measures with drugs and I am given to understand that she is slightly better. I should like you to watch her, Druce, and give me your true opinion, quite frankly."

There was something in his tone which caused me to look at him uneasily.

"Are you keeping anything back?" I asked.

"Yes and no." was his answer. "I don't understand a healthy English girl being shattered by nerves and" – he sprang to his feet as he spoke – "she is hand and glove with Mme. Sara."

"What!" I cried.

"She owns to the act and glories in it. Madame has cast her accustomed spell over her. I warned Lady Bouverie on no account to consult her medically, and she promised. But, there, how far is a woman's word, under given circumstances, to be depended upon?"

"Violet would certainly keep her word." I answered, in a tone almost of indignation.

He shrugged his shoulders.

"Your friend Violet is human" he answered. "She is losing her looks; she gets thinner and older-looking day by day. Under such circumstances any woman who holds the secrets Mme. Sara does would compel another to be guided by her advice. At present Sir John has not the slightest idea that Lady Bouverie consulted me, but if you have any reason to fear that Madame is treating her we must tell him the truth at once. I have opened your eyes. You will, I am sure, do what is necessary."

He left me a few minutes later and I sat by the fire pondering over his words.

Sir John Bouverie was a man of considerable note. He was a great deal older than his young wife and held a high position in the foreign office.

I reached Greylands the next morning soon after breakfast to find the country bathed in sunshine, the air both crisp and warm, and on the lawn the dew glistening like myriads of sparkling gems.

Sir John gave me a hearty welcome; he told me that Violet had not yet come downstairs and then hurried me to my room to change and join the day's shooting party.

We had excellent sport and did not reach home again until 5 o'clock. Lady Bouverie and several guests were at tea in the library. Although Vandeleur had in a measure prepared me for a grate change in her appearance, I was shocked and startled when I saw her. As a girl Violet had been bright, upright, dark of eye with a vivid color and an off-hand, dashing, joyous sort of manner. A perfect radiance of life seemed to emanate from her. To be in her presence was to be assured of a good time, so merry was her laugh, so contagious her high spirits. Now she looked old, almost haggard, her color gone, her eyes tired, dull and sunken. She was scarcely 20 yet, but had anyone spoken of her as a woman past 30 the remark would provoke no denial.

Just for a moment as our eyes met hers brightened and a vivid, beautiful color filled her cheeks.

"This is good!" she cried. "I am so glad you have come! It will be like old times to have a long talk with you, Dixon. Come over now to this cozy nook by the fire and let us begin at once."

She crossed the room as she spoke and I followed her.

"All my guests have had tea, or if they have not they will help themselves." She continued. "Muriel, "she added, addressing a pretty girl in a white tea gown, who stood near, "help everyone, won't you. I am so excited at seeing my old friend, Dixon Druce again. Now then, Dixon, let us step back a few years into the sunny past. Don't you remember---------"

She plunged into old recollections and as she did so the animation in her sweet eyes and the color in her cheeks removed a good deal of the painful impression which her first appearance had given me. We talked, Lady Bouverie laughed, and all went well until I suddenly made an inquiry with regard to Hubert.

Now Hubert had been the darling of Violet's early life. He was about three years older her senior, and as fascinating and gay and light-hearted a young fellow as I had ever seen.

Violet turned distinctly pale when I spoke of him now. She was silent for a few minutes then she raised her eyes appealingly and said in a clear distinct voice;

"Hubert is quite well, I believe. Of course, you remember that he was obliged to go to Australia on business just before my marriage, but I hear from him constantly."

"I should have thought he would have been back by now," was my answer, "What has he done with the bungalow?"

"Let it to a very special friend. She goes there for week-ends. You must have heard of her — Mme. Sara."

"Oh, my dear Violet," I could not help saying, "why did Hubert let the place to her, of all people?"

"Why not?" was her answer. She started as she spoke. "I am very fond of Mme. Sara. Bud do you know her? You look as though you did."

"Too well," I replied.

Her lips pouted.

"I see this is a subject on which we are not likely to agree," She answered. "I love Madame, and for that matter, so does Hubert. I never met anyone who had such an influence over him. Sometimes I think that if she were a little younger and he a little older ----but, there, of course, his devotion to her is not of that kind. She can do anything with him however. He went to Australia entirely to please her. How strange you look. Have I said too much? But, there, I must not talk to you any more for the present. The fascination of your company has made me 'forget my other duties."

She left me, and I, presently found myself in my own room, where, seated by the fire, I thought over matters. I did not like the aspect of affairs. The Willow let to Mme. Sara; Hubert in Australia and evidently on Madame's business; could Violet's all too manifest trouble have anything to do with Hubert? Her manner by no means deceived me; she was concealing something. How ill she looked; how changed. Those forced spirits, that struggle to be animated did not for a single moment blind me to the true fact that Violet was unhappy.

At dinner that evening I again noticed young Lady Bouverie's tired and yet excited appearance. Once her dark eyes met mine; but she looked away immediately. She was in distress. What could be wrong?

It was one of Sir John's peculiarities to sit up very late, and that night after the ladies had retired to rest we went into the billiard room. After indulging in a couple of games I lit a fresh cigar, and, feeling the air of the room somewhat hot, stepped out onto the wide veranda, which happened to be deserted. I had taken one or two turns when I heard the rustle of a dress behind me, and turning, saw Violet. She was wearing a long, straight, rather heavy, pearl-gray velvet dress which I had admired and yet thought too old for her, earlier in the evening. She came up eagerly by my side. As I had

Bidden her good night a long time ago I could not help showing my astonishment.

"Don't look at me with those shocked, reproachful eyes, Dixon," She said in a low voice. "I am lucky to catch you like this. I want to speak to you about something."

"Don't Look at Me With Those Reproachful Eyes, Dixon."

"Certainly," I replied. "Shall we go over to those chairs, or will you feel it too cold?"

"Not at all. Yes. Let us go over there." I drew forward one of the chairs at the corner of the veranda, wondering greatly what was coming.

Lady Bouverie looked up at me as I stood by her side, with some of the old, frank expression in her brown eyes.

"Dixon," she said, "I want you to help me and not to question me; whatever your private thoughts may be I want you to keep them to yourself. This is a most private and important matter, and I demand your help to get me through satisfactorily."

"You have only to command," I replied.

As I spoke I glanced at her anxiously. The moonlight had caught her face, and I saw how deadly white she was. Her lips quivered. Suddenly her eyes filled with tears. She took out a tiny lace handkerchief and wiped them away. In a moment she had recovered her self-control and continued'

"I am in great trouble just now, and the bitter part of it is that I can confide it to no one. But I want you, as an old friend, to do a little business for me. I can't manage it myself, or I would not ask you. I have not told my husband anything about it, nor do I wish him to know. It is not my duty to tell him, for the affair is my own, not his. You understand?"

"No," I answered boldly. "I cannot understand any circumstances in which a wife could rightly have a trouble apart from her husband."

"Oh, don't be so goody-goody, Dixon, "she said, with some petulance. "If you won't help me without lecturing, you are much changed from the old Dixon Druce who used to give us such jolly times when he called himself our dear old uncle at the Willows. Say at once whether you will go right on with this thing, or whether I shall get someone else to do what I require."

I thought of Madame, who would not scruple to do anything to get this girl into her power.

"Of course I will help you," I said. "We will leave out the goody part and go straight to business. What is it?"

"Now you are nice and like your own self," she replied. "Please listen attentively. I have in my private box some rupee coupon bonds, payable to bearer. These I inherited among other securities at my mother's death. I want to realize them into cash immediately. I could not do so personally without my husband's knowledge, as I should have to correspond with or go to see the family broker in the city. Now, I want you to sell them for me at the best price. I know the price is low owing to the fall in silver, but as they are bearer bonds there will be no transfer deeds to sign, and you can take them to your broker and get the money at once. Can you do this for me tomorrow? I hate asking you, but if you would do it I should be so grateful. The fact is, I must somehow have the money before tomorrow night."

"I will certainly do it," I replied. "I can run up to town tomorrow morning on the plea of urgent business, which will be quite true, and bring you back the money tomorrow afternoon."

Her words had filled me with apprehension, but it was quite impossible after what she had just said, to attempt to gain her confidence as to the cause of her wish for a sudden supply of cash unknown to her husband. Could she want the money for Hubert? But he was in Australia.

"Is the amount a large one?" I asked.

"Not very, "she answered. "I think the bonds should realize, at the present price, about £2600."

"Indeed!" I exclaimed. "That appears to me a large sum."

The amount doubled my anxiety. A sudden impulse seized me.

"We are old friends, Violet," I said, laying my hand on her arm. "You and Hubert and I once swore eternal friendship. Now because of that old friendship, I will do what you ask, though I don't like to do it, and I would rather your husband knew about it. Since this is not to be, I mean to put to you another question, and I demand, Violet – yes, I demand – a frank answer."

"What is it?" she asked.

"Has Mme. Sara anything, directly or indirectly, to do with this affair?"

She glanced at me in astonishment.

"Mme. Sara. Absolutely nothing! Why should she?"

"Have you consulted her about it?"

"Well, yes, I have, of course. She is you see, my very kindest friend."

"And you are doing this by her advice?"

I was silent. My consternation was too great for me to but into words.

"Violet," I said, after a pause, "I am sorry that Madame has got possession of your dear old home; I am sorry you are friends with her; I am more than sorry you consult her, for I do not like her."

"Then you are in the minority, Dixon. All people praise Mme. Sara. She makes friends wherever she goes."

"Ah," I answered, "except with the few who know her as she is. Ask Vandeleur what he thinks of her."

155

"I admire Mr. Vandeleur very much," said Violet, speaking slowly. "He is a clever and interesting man, but were he to abuse Madame I should hate him. I could even hate you, Dixon, when you speak as you are now doing. It is, of course, because you know Mr. Vandeleur so well. He is a police official, a sort of detective --- such people look on all the world with jaundiced eyes. He would be sure to suspect any very clever woman."

"Vandeleur has told me," I said, after a pause, "that you respect and trust him sufficiently to consult him about your health."

"Yes," she answered. "I have not been feeling well. I happened to be alone with him on one occasion, and it seemed a chance not to be thrown away. He did look so clever and so—so trustworthy. He is giving me some medicines – I think I am rather better since I took them."

She gave a deep sigh and rose to her feet.

"Heigh-ho!" she said. "I had no idea it was so late. We must go in. John sits up till all hours. Good night and a thousand thanks. I will put the parcel of bonds in your room tomorrow morning, in the top left-hand drawer of the chest. You will know where to find them before you go to town."

She pressed my hand, and I noticed that there were tears brimming in her eyes. Her whole attitude puzzled me terribly. It was so unlike the ways of the Violet I used to know. Fearless, bold, daring was that girl. I used to wonder at times could she ever cry; could she ever feel keen anxiety about anyone? Now, only six months after marriage, I found a nervous, almost hypochondriacal woman instead of the Violet of old.

I thought much of Lady Bouverie's request during the hours of darkness; and in the morning notwithstanding the fact that in some way it might be considered a breach of confidence, I resolved to tell Vandeleur. Vandeleur would keep the knowledge to himself; unless, indeed, it was for Lady Bouverie's benefit that he should disclose it. I felt certain that she was in grave danger of some sort, and, knowing Mme. Sara as I did, my apprehensions flew to her as the probable cause of the trouble.

After breakfast I made an excuse and went up to town, taking the bonds with me.

Just as I was entering my broker's I observed a man leaning against the railings. He was dressed like an ordinary tramp, and had a slouched hat pushed over his eyes. Those eyes, very bright and watchful, seemed to haunt me. I did not think they looked like the eyes of an English-man –they were too brilliant and also too secretive.

My broker gave me an open check for £2,600 for the bonds. This I at once took to his bank and cashed in notes. As I was leaving the bank I observed the same man whom I had seen standing outside the broker's office. He did not look at me this time, but sauntered slowly by. I was conscious of a curious, irritated feeling, and had some difficulty in banishing him from my mind. That he was following me I had little doubt, and this fact doubled my uneasiness.

I got into a cab and drove to Vandeleur's house, when I arrived there were no signs of the man. And, blaming myself for being over scrupulous I inquired for my friend. He was out, but I was lucky enough to catch him just outside the court. He was very busy and could only give me a moment. I told him my news briefly. His face grew grave.

"Bad," Was his laconic remark. "I told you I feared there was something going on. I wonder what Lady Bouverie is up to?"

"Nothing dishonorable," I replied hotly. "Do you think, Vandeleur, she wants the money for her brother?"

"Hubert Sale has plenty of money of his own," was Vandeleur's retort. "Besides, you say he is in Australia — gone on Mme. Sara's business. I don't like it Druce. Believe me, Sara is at the bottom of this. You must watch for all you are worth. You must get the detective. Never mind whether you like the part or not. It is for the sake of that poor girl. She has beyond doubt put herself in the clutches of the most dangerous woman in London."

Vandeleur's remarks were certainly not encouraging. I returned to Greylands in low spirits. Lady Bouverie was waiting for me on the lawn; the rest of the party were out. She looked tired; the ravages of some secret grief were more than manifest on her face. But when I handed her the parcel of notes she gave me a look of gratitude and without speaking hurried to her own apartments.

I was just preparing to saunter through the grounds, feeling too restless to go within, when a light hand was laid on my arm. Lady Bouverie had returned.

"I could not wait Dixon," she cried. "I had to thank you at once. You are good, and you have done better than I dared to hope. Now I shall be quite, quite happy. This must put everything absolutely right. Oh, the relief! I was not meant for anxiety; I believe much of it would kill me."

"I am inclined to agree with you," I answered looking at her face as I spoke.

"Ah," She answered, "you think me greatly changed?"

"I do."

"You will soon see the happy Violet of old. You have saved me. You are going for a walk. May I accompany you?"

I assured her what pleasure it would give me and we went together through the beautiful gardens. Her whole manner only strengthened my anxiety. Mme. Sara, her great and trusted friend; a large sum of money required immediately which her husband was to know nothing about; Hubert Sale at the other side of the world, engaged on Mme. Sara's business; Madame in possession of the Sales' old home. Things looked bleak.

Sir John had asked me to remain at Greylands for a fortnight and I resolved for Violet's sake to take full advantage of the invitation.

Our party was a gay one, and perhaps I was the only person who really noticed Violet's depression.

Meantime there was great excitement for a large house party was expected to arrive, the chief guest being a certain Persian, Mr. Mirza All Khan, one of the shah's favorite courtiers, and most trusted emissaries. This great personage had come to England to prepare for his royal master's visit to this country, the –date of which was as yet uncertain. Sir John Bouverie, by virtue of his official position at the foreign office had offered to entertain him for a few days shooting.

"I do not envy Ali Khan is billet," remarked Sir John to me on the evening before the arrival of our honored guest. "The shah is a particular monarch, and if everything is not in apple-pie order on his arrival there is certain to be big trouble for someone. In fact, if the smallest thing goes wrong, Mirza Ali Khan is likely to lose his head when he returns to Persia. My guest of tomorrow has a very important commission to execute before the shah's arrival. Amongst some valuable gems and stones which he is bringing to have cut and set for his monarch, in especial, the bloodstone"

"What?" I asked.

"The bloodstone. The bloodstone, which has never before left Persia. It is the shah's favorite talisman, and is supposed among other miraculous properties, to possess the power of rendering the royal owner invisible at will. Awful thing if he were suddenly to disappear at one of the big court functions. But, to be serious, the stone is intensely interesting for its grate age and history, having been the most treasured possession of the Persian court for untold centuries. Though I believe it is intrinsically worth very little, its sentimental value is enormous. Were it lost, a huge reward would be offered for it. It has never been set, but is to be so now for the first time and is to b ready for the shah to wear on his arrival. It will be a great honor to handle and examine a stone with such a history and Violet has asked the Persian to bring it down here as a special favor, in order that we may all see it."

"It will be most interesting," I replied. Then I added: "Surely there must be an element of risk in the way these eastern potentates bring their priceless stones and jewels with them when they visit our western cities, the feel of all the great professional thieves of the world?"

"Very little," He replied. "The home office is always specially notified, and they pass the word to Scotland Yard, so that every precaution is taken."

He rose as he spoke and we both joined the other men in the billiard room.

On the following day the new guests arrived. They had come by special train and in time for tea, which was

160

served in the central hall. Among them, of course, was the Persian, Mirza Ali Khan. He was a fine looking man, handsome with lustrous dark eyes and a clear-cut high bred features. His manners were extremely polite, and he abundantly possessed all an easterner's grace and charm. I had been exchanging a few words with him, and was turning away when, to my absolute surprise and consternations, I found myself face to face with Mme. Sara. She was standing close behind me, stirring her tea. She still wore her hat and cloak, as did all the other ladies who had just arrived.

"Ah, Mr. Druce," she cried, a brilliant smile lighting up her face and displaying her dazzling white teeth, "so we meet again. Dear me, you look surprised and – scarcely pleased to see me."

She dropped her voice.

"You have no cause to be alarmed," she continued. "I am not a ghost."

"I did not know you were to be one of Sir John's guests tonight," I answered.

"In your opinion I ought not to be, ought I? But, you see, dear Lady Bouverie is my special friend. In spite of many professional engagements I determined to give her the pleasure of my society tonight. I wanted to spend a short time with her in her beautiful home and still more I wished to meet one again that fascinating Persian, Mr. Kahn. You don't believe me, I know, Mr. Druce, when I tell you that I knew him as a boy. I was at Teheran for a time many years ago and I was a special friend of the late shah's."

"You know the late shah!" I exclaimed, staring at her in undisguised amazement.

"Yes; I spent nearly a year in Persia, and can talk the language quite fluently. Ah!"

She turned away and addressed herself evidently in his own language, to the Persian. A pleased and delighted smile spread over his dark oriental features. He extended his hand to her, and the next moment they were exchanging a rapid conversation, much to the surprise of all. Lady Bouverie looked on at this scene. Her eyes were bright with excitement. I noticed that she kept gazing at Mme. Sara as though fascinated. Presently she turned to me.

"Is she not wonderful?" she exclaimed. "Think of her adding Persian to her many accomplishments. She is so wonderfully brilliant – she makes everything go well. There certainly is no one like her."

"No one more dangerous," I could not help whispering.

Violet shrugged her pretty shoulders.

"There never was anyone more obstinate and prejudiced than you can be when you like, Dixon," she answered. "Ah, there is Madame calling me. She and I mean to have a cozy hour in my boudoir before dinner."

She flew from my side and as I stood in the hall I saw the young hostess and Mme. Sara going slowly up the wide stairs side by side. I thought how well Violet looked, and began to hope that her trouble was at an end—that the money I had brought her had done what she hoped it would, and that Madame for the time was innocuous.

But I was destined to be quickly undeceived. About an hour later I was standing in one of the corridors, when Violet Bouverie ran past me. She pulled herself up the next instant and, turning, came up to me on tiptoe. Her face was so changed that I should scarcely have recognized it.

"The worst has happened," she said, in a whisper.

"What do you mean?" I asked.

"Hubert—I did think I could save him. Oh, I am nearly mad."

"Madame has brought you bad tidings?"

"The worst. What am I to do? I must keep up appearances tonight. Don't take any notice of me; I will tell you tomorrow. But heaven help me! Heaven help me!" she sobbed.

"Heaven Help Me," She Sobbed.

I watched her as she walked quickly down the corridor. Her handkerchief was pressed to her face; tears were streaming from her eyes. Hatred even stronger than I had ever seen before experienced filled me with regard to Mme. Sara. My first impulse was to herd the lioness in her den, to demand an interview with the woman, tell her all my suspicions, and dare her to torture Violet Bouverie any further. But reflection showed me the absurdity of this plan. I must wait and watch; ah yes. I would watch, even as a detective, and would not leave a stone unturned to pursue this terrible woman until her wicked machinations were laid bare.

IT was with a sinking heart that I dressed for dinner, but by and by, when I found myself at the long table, with its brilliant decorations and its distinguished guests, and glanced round the glittering board, I almost wondered if all that I had felt and all that Violet Bouverie's face had expressed were not parts of a hideous dream; for the party was so gay, the conversation so full of wit and laughter, that surely no horrible tragedy could be lingering in the background.

But as these thoughts came to me I looked again at Violet. At tea time that evening I had noticed her improved appearance, but now she looked ghastly; her cheeks were hollow, her eyes sunken, her complexion a dull, dead white. Her evening dress revealed hollows in her neck. But it was the tired look, the suppressed anguish on her face, which filled me with apprehension. I could see how bravely she tried to be bright and gay. I also noticed that her eyes avoided mine.

Burza Ali Khan sat on the right of Lady Bouverie — on his other side sat Mme. Sara, and I occupied a chair next to hers. Between Madame and our hostess appeared tonight a most marked and painful contrast. Violet Bouverie was not 20. Mme. Sara, by her own showing, was an old woman, and yet at that moment the old looked young and the young old. Madam's face was brilliant, not a wrinkle was to be observed; her make-up was so perfect that it could not be detected even by the closest observer. Her tout ensemble gave her the appearance of a woman who could not be a day more than 25. Many a man would have fallen a victim to her wit and brilliancy; but I at least was saved that—I knew her too well. I hated her for that beauty, which affected such havoc in the world.

It was easy to see that Ali Khan was fascinated by her; but at the table she had the good taste to address him in English. Now and then I noticed that she looked earnestly at our hostess. After one of these glances she turned to me and said in a low voice:

"How ill Lady Bouverie is looking! Don't you think so?"

"Yes, "I replied, "she is. I feel anxious about her."

"I wish she would consult me," She replied. "I could do her good. But she will not. She is under the impression Mr. Druce, that I am a quack because I do not hold diplomas—a curious delusion I find among people."

"But a smart one," I answered.

She laughed and turned again to her other neighbor.

When we joined the ladies after dinner Lady Bouverie crossed over to the Persian and said something to him.

"Certainly," he answered, and immediately left the room, returning in a few minutes with a dispatch box. We all clustered about him as he placed it on the table and opened it. A little murmur of surprise ran round the group when he lifted the lid and displayed the contents. A mass of gorgeous gems was lying in a bed of white wool. It was a blaze of all the colors of the rainbow. Emeralds, sapphires, diamonds, rubies, pearls, topazes, cats'—eyes, amethysts and many others whose names I did not know were to be found there. One by one he removed and passed each round for inspection. As he did so he gave a short description of its virtues, its origin, and value, and then returned it to the box again. Truly the display was wonderful. Mme. Sara lingered long and lovingly over some of the gems, declaring that she had seen one or two before, mentioning certain anecdotes about them to the Persian, who nodded and smiled as he replaced, with his pointed fingers, each in its receptacle. He was evidently much pleased with the admiration they excited.

"But surely Mr. Khan, you have brought the bloodstone to show us?" questioned Lady Bouverie.

"Ah, yes, I kept that supreme treasure for the last."

As he spoke he pushed a spring in the box and a secret triangular drawer came slowly out. In it, nestling in a bed of red velvet, lay a wonderful stone – a perfectly oval piece of moss-green chalcedony with translucent edges. Here and there an irregular pattern shone out in vivid contrast to the dark green a number of blood-red spots from which the stone derived its name.

"Yes," He said, lifting it out with reverence and laying it on the palm of his hand. "This is the bloodstone. Look closely at it if you will, but I must ask none of you to touch it."

"I Must Ask None of You to Touch It."

One after another we bent down and peered into its luminous green depths and doubtless shared some of the fascination that its possessor must feel for it. The stone was wonderful, and yet it was repellant. It seemed to me that there was something sinister in those blood-red spots. The thing inspired me with the same feeling that I often have when regarding some monstrous spotted orchid.

"Yes," said Lady Bouverie. "It is wonderful. Tell us something of its history Mr. Khan."

"I cannot," he answered. "for the simple reason that no one knows its origin or when it came into the possession of our court. I could tell of some of its properties, but the tales would fall unassumingly on the ears of western civilization."

He replaced the stone in its drawer and, in spite of our pleading, declined to discuss it further.

It was late that night before I retired to rest. I was sitting with my host in the smoking room and we walked together down the corridor which led to my room. Most of the lights in the houses were already out, and I fancied as I chatted to Bouverie that I heard a door close softly just ahead of us. The next instant, glancing down, I saw on the dark carpet a piece of paper open and bearing traces of having been folded. It was obviously a note.

"Halloa!" cried Bouverie. "What is this?"

He stopped and picked it up. At a glance we both read its contents they read as follows:

"Bring it to the summer house exactly at 12:30; but make certain that Dixon Druce has retired. Don't come until he has."

Bouverie's eyes met mine. I could not tell what thoughts flashed into their brown depths; but the rosy hue suddenly left her face, leaving it deadly white.

"Do you understand this?" he said, addressing me briefly.

"Yes and no," I replied.

"For whom was this note intended?" was his next remark.

I was silent.

"Druce," said Bouverie, "are you hiding anything from me?"

"If I were you, "I said, after a moment's quick thought, "I would attend that rendezvous. It is now 25 minutes past 12" —I glanced at my watch as I spoke--- "Shall we go together?"

He nodded. I rushed to my room, put on a dark shooting coat, and joined my host a moment later in the hall.

We slipped out through a side door which stood slightly open. Without a word we crept softly in the shadow of the bushes towards the summer house at the farther end of the garden which was clearly visible in the moonlight. Whatever thoughts were coursing through Bouverie's brain, there was something about his attitude, a certain forceful determination, which kept him from any words. We both drew into the dark cover of the laurels and waited with what patience we could.

A moment had scarcely gone by when across the grass with a light, quick step came a woman. She was wrapped in a dark cloak. For one instant the moonlight fell on her face, and my heart nearly stopped with horror. It was that of Lady Bouverie. At that instant Bouverie's hand clutched my shoulder, and he drew me farther back into the darkest part of the shadow. From where we stood we could see but not be seen. Lady Bouverie was holding a small box in one hand, in the other a handkerchief. Her eyes were streaming with tears. She had scarcely reached the summer house before a man with a mask over his face approached her. He said a word or two in a whisper which was only broken by Lady Bouverie's sobs. She gave him the box; he put it into his breast pocket and vanished.

I wondered that Bouverie did not spring forward, seize the man and demand an explanation; but whether he was stunned or not I could not say. Before, however, he made the slightest movement Lady Bouverie herself, with incredible swiftness, disappeared into the darkness.

"Come," I said to Bouverie.

We both rushed to the spot where his wife had stood — something white lay on the ground. I picked it up. It was her handkerchief. Bouverie snatched it from me and looked at the initials by the light of the moon. The handkerchief was sopping wet with tears. He flung it down again as though it hurt him.

"Great heavens!" he muttered.

I picked up the handkerchief and we both returned to the house.

We had scarcely set food inside the hall when the sound of many voiced upstairs fell on our ears. Amongst them the Persian's accents were clearly distinguishable. Terror rang in every shrill word.

"The bloodstone is gone! — the other jewels are safe, but the bloodstone, the talisman, is gone! What will become of me? My life will be on the forfeit."

We both rushed upstairs. The whole thing was perfectly true. The bloodstone, the priceless talisman of the royal house of Persia, had been stolen. The confusion was appalling, and already someone had gone to fetch the local police.

"I shall lose my life if the stone is not recovered," Cried the miserable Persian, despair and terror depicted on his face. "Who has taken it? The other gems are safe, but the secret drawer has been burst open and the bloodstone removed. Who has taken it? Sir John, what is the matter? You look strange."

170

"I can throw light on this mystery," said Sir John.

I looked around me. Neither Lady Bouverie nor Mme. Sara was present. I felt a momentary thankfulness for this latter fact.

"I saw my wife give a package to a stranger in the garden just now," he continued. "I do not wish to conceal anything. This matter must be looked into. When the police come I shall be the first to help in the investigation. Meanwhile I am going to my wife."

He strode away. We all stood and looked at each other. Sir John's revelation was far more terrible to all except the unfortunate Persian than the loss of the bloodstone. In fact, the enormity of the one tragedy paled beside the other.

I thought for a minute, notwithstanding the intense of the hour, I would dispatch a telegram to Vandeleur without delay. There was a mystery, and only Vandeleur could clear it up. Black as appearances were against Lady Bouverie, I had no doubt that her innocence could be established. Without a word I hurried out and raced up to the post office. There I knocked up the postmaster and soon dispatched three telegrams — one to Vandeleur's house, one to his club, and one to the care of the Westminster police station. All contained the same words:

"Come special or motor immediately. Don't delay."

I then returned to Greylands. A hush of surprise had succeeded to the first consternation. A few of the guests had reappeared, startled by the noise and confusion, but many still remained in their rooms. Sir John was with his wife. We assembled in the dining room and presently he came down and spoke to us.

"Lady Bouverie denies everything," he said. "She swears she has never left her room. This matter must be thoroughly investigated," he continued, going up to the Persian. "There are times when a man in all honor cannot defend even his own wife."

Meanwhile Mme. Sara remained in the library. She was sitting by a table busily writing. When Sir John appeared she came into the room and spoke to him. Her face was full of sympathy.

"Of course Violet is innocent," she said, "I cannot understand your story, Sir John."

He did not reply to her. She then offered to go up to Violet; but he peremptorily forbade her to do so.

On the arrival of the local police a formal inquiry was made. Mirza Ali Khan declared that after showing us the gems he returned the box to his room. On retiring for the night he observed that it had been moved from the position in which he had placed it. He examined it and found that the lock had been tampered with – had; indeed, been ruthlessly, burst open, evidently with a blunt instrument. He then touched the spring which revealed the secret drawer — the bloodstone was gone. All the other gems were intact. Knowing that the secret of the drawer was a difficult one to discover, the Persian was convinced that the bloodstone had been stolen by one of the party who assembled round him that evening and who had seen him touch the spring.

"My host, Sir John Bouverie, tells me an incredible story," he said. "I will leave the matter in Sir John's hands, trusting absolutely to his honor."

In a few words Sir John described what he had seen. He handed the note, which we had found in the corridor to the police, who examined it with interest. Lady Bouverie was sent for, and pending further investigation the unfortunate girl was placed under arrest.

Half past 1 struck, then 2 and it was only our earnest appeal to await Vandeleur's arrival that prevented the police from removing Lady Bouverie in custody. Would he never come? If he had started at once on receipt of the wire he would be nearly at Greylands now.

Suddenly I heard a sound and ran breathlessly to the front door, which was open. Stepping from a motor car, hatless but with the utmost calm, was Vandeleur. I seized his hand.

"Thank heaven you are here!" I exclaimed. "You must have raced."

"Yes, I shall be summoned tomorrow for fast driving, and I have lost my hat. What's up?"

I hurried him into the dining room where a crowd of guests was assembled. It was a wonderful scene and I shall never forget it. The anxious faces of the visitors; Lady Bouverie standing between two constables, sobbing bitterly; her husband, just behind her, his head turned with shame and misery; and then, as though in contrast, the tall commanding figure of Vandeleur, with his strong features set as though in marble. He was taking in everything, judging in his acute mind the evidence, which was poured out to him.

"Have you anything to say?" asked Vandeleur, gently, to Lady Bouverie. "Any explanation to offer?"

"I was not there," was her answer. "I never left my room."

The rest of guests were ordered away, Mme. Sara taking herself off, though I could see that she went unwillingly. Sir John Vandeleur, myself, the Persian, the two constables and Lady Bouverie were now alone.

Vandeleur's expression suddenly changed. He was regarding Lady Bouverie with a steady look, he then took up the handkerchief which we had, and found, examined it carefully laid it down again.

"Have you been taking the medicine I ordered you, Lady Bouverie?" was his remark.

"I have," she replied.

"Today?"

"Yes, three times."

"Will someone give me a large, clean sheet of white paper?"

I found one at once and brought it to him. He carefully rolled the handkerchief in it, drew out his stylograph, and wrote on the package.

"Handkerchief found by Sir John Bouverie and Mr. Druce at 12:40pm"

He then asked Lady Bouverie for the one which she had in her pocket; this was almost as wet as the one I had picked up. He put it in another packet, writing also upon the paper.

"Handkerchief given to me by Lady Bouverie at 3:20am."

Then, drawing the inspector aside he whispered a few words to him which brought forth an exclamation of surprise from that officer.

"Now," he said, turning to Sir John, "I have done my business here for the present. I mean to return to London at once in my motor car and I shall take Mr. Druce with me. The inspector here has given me leave to take also these two handkerchiefs on which I trust important evidence may hang."

He drew out his watch.

"It is now nearly 3:30" he said, "I shall reach my house at 4:30, the examination will take fifteen minutes, the result will be dispatched from Westminster police station to the station here by telegram. You should receive it, Sir John by 5:30, and I trust," he added taking Lady Bouverie's hand, "It will mean your release, for that you are guilty I do not for a moment believe. In the meantime the police will remain here."

He caught my arm, and two minutes later we were rushing through the night towards London.

Two Minutes Later We Were Rushing Through the Night.

"My dear fellow" I gasped, "explain yourself for heavens sake. Is Violet innocent?"

"Wonderful luck," was his enigmatical answer. "I fancy Sara has overacted this piece."

"You can find the bloodstone?"

"That I cannot tell you, my business is to clear Lady Bouverie. Don't talk or we shall be wrecked."

He did not vouchsafe another remark till we stood together in his room, but he had driven the car like a madman.

He then drew out the two packets containing the handkerchiefs and began to make rapid chemical preparations.

"Now, listen," he said. "You know I am treating Lady Bouverie. The medicine I have been giving her happens to contain large doses of iodide of potassium. You may not be aware of it, but the drug is eliminated very largely by all the mucous membranes, and the lachrymal gland, which secretes the tears, plays a prominent part in this process. The sobbing female whom you are prepared to swear on oath was Lady Bouverie at the rendezvous by the summer house dropped a handkerchief—this one." He laid his finger on the first of the two packets. "Now, if that woman was really Lady Bouverie, by analysis of the handkerchief I shall find, by means of a delicate test, distinct traces of iodine on it. If, however, it was not Lady Bouverie, but someone disguised with the utmost skill of an actress to represent her, not only physically, but with all the emotions of a distracted and guilty woman, even to the sobs and tears—then we shall not find iodine on the analysis of this handkerchief."

My jaw dropped as the meaning of his words broke upon me.

"The handkerchief taken from Lady Bouverie's room and marked with her initials was intended to be the finishing touch to the chain of evidence against her. Now we will come to facts, and for all our sakes let us hope that my little theory is correct."

He set to work rapidly. At the end of some operations lasting several minutes he held up a test tube containing a clear solution.

"Now," he said, opening a bottle containing a opalescent liquid; "guilty or not guilty?"

He added a few drops from the bottle to the testing tube. A long, deep chuckle came from his broad chest.

"Not a trace of it," he said. "Now for the handkerchief, which I took from Lady Bouverie for a check experiment."

He added a few of the same drops to another tube. A bright violet color spread through the liquid.

"There's iodine in that, you see. 'Not guilty, Druce."

A shout burst from my lips.

"Hush my dear chap!" he pleaded. "Yes it is very pretty. I am quite proud."

Five minutes later a joyful telegram was speeding on its way to Greylands.

"So it was Sara," I said, by-and-by.

"What is your next move?"

He shrugged his shoulders.

"It is one thing to prove that a person is not guilty, but it is another thing to prove that someone else is. Of course, I will try. This is the deepest game I ever struck, and the boldest, and I think the cleverest. Poor Ali Khan, the shah will certainly cut his head off when he gets back to Persia. Of course, Sara has taken the stone. But whether she has done so simply because she has a fancy to keep it for herself believing in its power as a talisman, or for the reward which is certain to be offered, who can tell? The reward will be a large on, but she doesn't want money. However, we shall see her make up was good, and she had all her details well worked out."

"But we have not yet found out what Violet's trouble is," I remarked. "There is, I am sure, some mystery attached to Hubert."

"I doubt it" said Vandeleur, brusquely. He rose and yawned.

"I am tired and must lie down "he said. "You will of course, return to Greylands later in the morning. Let me know if there are any fresh moves."

By noon that day I found myself back at Greylands. Surely this was a day of wonders, for whom should I see standing on the steps of the old house, talking earnestly to Sir John Bouverie, by my old friend, Hubert Sale. In appearance he was older than when I had last seen him, and his face was bronzed. He did not notice me, but went quickly into the house. Sir John came down the avenue to meet me.

"Ah, Druce," he said, "Who would have believed it? Of all the amazing things, your friend Vandeleur's penetration is the greatest. We both saw her with our own eyes, and yet it wasn't my wife. Come into my study, "he continued, "I believe I can throw light on this most extraordinary affair. Hubert's unlooked-for return puts the whole thing into a nutshell. I have a strange tale to tell you."

"First, may I ask one question?" I interrupted. "Where is Mme. Sara?"

He spread out his hands with a significant gesture.

"Gone," he said. "How, when, and where I do not know. We thought she had retired for the night. She did not appear this morning. She had vanished, leaving no address behind her."

"Just like her," I could not help saying. "Now I will listen to your story."

"I will try to put it in as few words as possible. It's a deep thing and discloses a plot the malignity of which could scarcely be equaled.

"Violet and Hubert made the acquaintance of Mme. Sara a few months before Violet's marriage. You know Madame's power of fascination. She won Violet's affections, and as to Hubert, she had such complete influence over him that he would do anything in the world she wished. We were surprised at his determination to go to Australia before his sister's wedding, but it now turns out that he was forced to go by Madame herself, who assured him that he could be of the utmost assistance to her in a special matter of business. This was explained to Violet and to me fully, but what we were not told was that he took with him Madame's own special servant, an Arabian of the name Achmed, the cleverest man, Hubert said, he had ever met. In his absence madam rented his house for at least a year. All this sounds innocent enough, but listen.

"Very shortly after her marriage Violet began to receive letters from Hubert dated from various stations in Australia demanding money. These demands were couched in such terms as to terrify the poor child. She send him what she could from her own supplies but he was insatiable. At last she spoke to Mme. Sara. Madame immediately told her she had learned that Hubert had made some bad companions, had got into serious scrapes and that his debts of honor were so enormous that unless she, Violet, helped him, he could never set foot in England again. The poor girl was too much ashamed to say a word to me. These letters imploring money came by almost every mail. Madame herself offered to transmit the money, and Violet, with the utmost confidence, placed large sums in her hands.

"At last the crisis arrived. A communication reached my poor girl to the effect that unless she paid between two and three thousand pounds in notes in a couple of days Hubert in his despair would certainly take his life. She was well aware of his somewhat reckless character. Hence her entreaty to you to sell the bonds. The Persian followed here, and Madame at her own request came to spend the night. She managed to terrify Violet with a fresh supply with regard to Hubert, and the child's nerves were so undermined that she believed everything.

"Well, you know the rest. You know what happened last night. But for Vandeleur's genius, where might poor Violet be now? I must tell you frankly that even I believed her guilty. I could not doubt the evidence of my own senses.

You can judge of our amazement when Hubert walked in this morning. He looked well. He said that Madame's business was of simple character that he had soon put matters right for her, and after seeing what was to be seen in Australia and New Zealand came home. He was amazed when we spoke of his being in money difficulties; he has never been in any scrape at al. Only one thing he could not understand — why Violet never answered his letters. He wrote to her about every second mailing and as a rule, gave his letters to the Arabian to post. There is no doubt that the Arabian destroyed them and wrote others on his own account.

"Well, Druce, what do you say? The motive? Oh, of course, the motive was the bloodstone. The woman knew probably for months that it was coming to England, and that

I, in my official position, would invite the Persian here. She wanted it, goodness knows for what, and was determined to have a long chain of evidence against poor Violet in order to over her own theft. Druce we must find that woman. She cannot possibly be at large any longer."

The desire to find Madame was in all our minds, but how to accomplish it was a question, which I for one did not dare to answer.

V. *The Teeth of the Wolf*

"I count on your accepting," said Vandeleur.

"But why?" I asked, with some impatience. "I have never heard anything favorable with regard to Mrs. Bensasan. Her cruelties to her animals are well known. Granted that she is the best tamer of wild animals in Europe, I would rather not know her."

"That has nothing to do with the case in point," replied Vandeleur. "Mrs. Bensasan and Madame Sara are working on one of Madame's worst plots. I have not the least doubt on the subject. It is my business to solve this mystery, and I want your aid."

"Of course, if you put it in that way I can refuse no longer," was my response. "But what do you mean?"

"Simply this" As Vandeleur spoke he leant back in his chair and drew a long puff from his meerschaum. "I am acting in the interests of Gerald Hilliers. You have, of course, heard of the missing girl?"

"Your enigmas become more and more puzzling," I replied. "I know but little of Gerald Hilliers. And who is the girl?"

"I have rather a pretty story to entertain you with. This is the state of things as nearly as I can narrate it. Mrs. Bensasan, the owner of Bensasan's menageries, is in some ways the talk of London. She has dared to do what hardly any other woman has done before her. She runs her shows herself, being always present at important exhibitions. Her lion-taming exploits were remarkable enough to arouse general attention in Paris last year, but now in London she is going on an altered tack. She is devoting herself to the training of even wilder and more difficult animals to manage—I mean wolves."

"But what about the girl and your friend Hilliers?"

"I will explain. But first let me tell you about Mrs. Bensasan. I must describe her before I go any farther. She is built on a very large scale, being six feet in height. She has strong features, prominent eyes and a ringing, harsh voice. Her mouth is remarkably large and wide. I understand that Madame Sara has supplied her with a perfect set of false teeth, so well made that they defy detection, but altogether she is disagreeable to look at although the very essence of strength. Now, this woman is a widow and has only one child of the name of Laura, a girl about 19 years of age, who is in all respects as unlike the mother as a daughter could be, for she is slight, fair and gentle-looking, with a particularly attractive face. Miss Laura has had the bad taste, according to Mrs. Bensasan, to fall in love with Hilliers, whereas the mother wants her for a very different bridegroom. I have known Hilliers for years, and his father is a friend of mine. He is a nice, gentlemanly fellow, with good commercial prospects. Now, although it is more than probable that Hilliers will be a rich man, Mrs. Bensasan does not wish for the match. She wants Laura to marry a horrible, misshapen little man – a dwarf of the name of Rigby. So far as I can ascertain, Rigby is half Jew, half Greek, and he has evidently known as Mrs. Bensasan for many years. He lives in an expensive lodging near Cavendish square, drives a small phaeton, and has all the externals that belong to a rich man. His face is as repulsive as his body is misshapen. The girl cannot stand him and what the mother sees in him is the most difficult part of the problem which I have got to solve. It may be a case of blackmail. If so, I must prove it. There is not the slightest doubt that this extremely strong and disagreeable woman fears Rigby, although she professes to be a great friend of his.

In addition, Madame Sara is Mrs. Bensasan's friend. She spends a great deal of her time at Cray Lodge, the pretty little place near Guildford, where the Bensasan's live. These two women are evidently hand in glove, and both have resolved to give the poor girl to Joe Rigby, as things are at present, Gerald Hillier's stands a poor chance of winning his bride."

"You say the girl is missing?"

"Yes. About a month ago Gerald wrote to Mrs. Bensasan asking her for Laura's hand. He had quite a civil letter in reply, stating that the matter required consideration and that just at present she would rather he did not pay his addresses to her daughter. Nevertheless, he received an invitation a few days later to stay at Cray Lodge.

"He arrived there, was treated with marked kindness and allowed to see Laura as much as he liked. The poor girl seemed sadly restrained and unhappy. One day when the two found themselves alone she told him that he had better give her up as she knew there was not the slightest chance of her being allowed to marry him; but she further added that

185

under no circumstances would she marry Rigby. As she uttered the words Mrs. Bensasan came into the room. To all appearance she had heard nothing. Hilliers left Cray Lodge that afternoon.

"Early the next morning he received a letter from Mrs. Bensasan asking him to come to her at once. He hurried to the lodge; he was received by his hostess, who told him that she had sent Laura from home, and that she did not intent to reveal her whereabouts until she had decided to give her as a bride to Joe Rigby or to him. She would not say at present which suitor she most favored; she only reserved to herself the absolute power to choose between them.

"Laura shall only marry the man I choose her to marry.' was her final announcement and then she added, 'In order to study your character, Mr. Hilliers, I again invite you to come her on a visit. My friend, Mr. Rigby will also be a guest.'

"This state of things alone would have made Hilliers anxious, although not greatly alarmed, but Laura's old nurse, who had been hiding behind a laurustinus bush in the avenue, rushed up to him as he was returning to the railway station and thrust a note into his hand. It was written by herself and was very illiterate. In this she managed to inform him that her young lady had been removed from her bed in the middle of the night and been put forcibly in to a cab by Mrs. Bensasan and Madame Sara. It was the nurse's impression that the poor girl was about to be subjected to some very cruel treatment.

"Laura's Old Nurse Thrust a Note Into His Hand."

"Hilliers came to me at once and implored me to help him to find and rescue Miss Bensasan. I must own that I was at first puzzled how to act. It was just then that an extraordinary thing happened. Mrs. Bensasan came to see me. Her ostensible reason was to consult me with regard to some curious robberies which had lately taken place on her premises. Her great fear was that the people who committed the burglaries would try to injure her wolves by throwing poisoned meat to them. She had heard of me and my professional skill from her great friend Madame Sara, and in short, she wanted to know if I would take up the matter, insinuating that I should be handsomely paid for my services, and further, that I might bring my friend, Mr. Dixon Druce, with me.

"Madame Sara and I would like to have you both staying at Cray Lodge,' she said. 'I hope you will come. Will you, in company with your friend Mr. Druce, visit me next Monday? We can then go carefully into the matter and you can give me your opinion. It would be a most serious thing for me more serious than I can give you the least idea of, if my wolves were tampered with. I ask for your presence as a great favor. Will you both come?' "

"And you accepted that sort of invitation?" was my remark.

"I accepted it," replied Vandeleur gravely, "for us both".

"But why? Your attitude in this matter puzzles me very much. I should imagine that you would not care to darken that woman's doors."

"I suspect," said Vandeleur slowly, "that the tale of the robberies is a mere blind. I look forward to a very interesting time at Cray Lodge, for I intend to become possessed of the necessary knowledge which will enable me to give Miss Laura to Gerald Hilliers as his bride."

I greatly disliked the idea of going to stay at Cray Lodge. I thought Vandeleur was on the wrong track when entered Mrs. Bensasan's house as her guest. There was no help for it, however; he was determined to go and I, as his special friend, would not fail him in what was extremely likely to be an hour of danger.

On the following Monday accordingly I accompanied Vandeleur to Mrs. Bensasan's house. A smart dog-cart was waiting for us at Guildford and we drove to the lodge, a pretty house, situated about three miles out of town. It stood in its own grounds. There was a pine wood to the left, and I might have thought I was approaching one of the most innocent and lovely homes of England but for the sinister bay of a wolf that fell upon my ears as we drove up the avenue.

Tea was in full progress in the central hall when we arrived. Mrs. Bensasan wore a gown of tawny velvet, which suited her massive figure and harsh, yet in some ways handsome, face. Her hair was a shade redder in tone than the velvet, and she had it arranged in thick coils round her large head. Her dead-white complexion was unrelieved by any color. Her reddish eyebrows were thick, and her eyes, large and the color of agates, gleamed with approval as we entered the hall. She came forward at once to meet us.

"Welcome!" she said, in her harsh voice and as she spoke she smiled, showing those white, regular teeth which Vandeleur had mentioned as the work of that genius, Madame Sara.

We stood for a moment or two by the fire, and as we did so I watched her face. The brow was low, the eyes very large and very brilliant, but I thought them altogether destitute of humanity. The nose was thick with wide nostrils and the mouth was hideous, cut like a slit across her face. Notwithstanding her beautiful teeth, that mouth destroyed all pretense to good looks.

In the presence of one so coarse and colossal Madame Sara, who was standing in the background, appeared at first almost significant, but a second glance showed that this woman was the very foil she needed to bring out her remarkable and great attractions. Her slenderness and her young figure, the softness of her blue eyes, the golden sheen of that marvelous hair, which was neither dyed nor artificially curled, but was Nature's pure product, glistening and twining

189

itself into tendrils long, thick and soft as a girl's all contrasted well with the heavy appearance of her hostess. Mrs. Bensasan looked almost an old woman. Madame Sara might have been 28 or 80. She wore a black dress of cobwebby lace, and nothing could better suit the delicacy of her complexion.

I had just taken my second cup of tea when a voice at my elbow caused me to turn round quickly. Then indeed, I could not help startling, for one of the most misshapen and altogether horrible looking men I had ever seen stood before me. His face was all hillocks and excrescences the forehead bulging forward, the eyes going back very deeply into their sockets; they were small eyes and seemed ever to glisten with an uneasy and yet watchful movement. The lower part of his face was covered with a thick black moustache and short beard. The nose was small, very retrousse, with wide nostrils. Mrs. Bensasan introduced him with a careless nod.

"My friend, Mr. Joe Rigby — Mr. Druce" she said.

Rigby bowed rather offensively low, and then began to talk.

"I am glad you and Mr. Vandeleur are going to give us the pleasure of your company for a day or two," he said. "Mrs. Bensasan has a very fine scheme for our amusement on Wednesday night. You have, of course, heard of Mrs. Bensasan's wolves? I doubt not she will let you see them if you ask her. She is very proud of these animals, and no wonder. Taganrog, a great Siberian he-wolf, is alone likely to make her famous. It is Mrs. Bensasan's most kind intention to give us an exhibition of her power over Taganrog on Wednesday night."

"Indeed," I answered, "That will be interesting."

Someone called him and he moved away. Tea was over, but there were still a couple of hours of daylight left. Mrs. Bensasan stood a little apart from her other guests. She saw me and came up to my side.

"Should you be afraid if I took you to see my pets?" she said.

"I should like to go very much," I replied.

"You are certain you will not turn coward? Some people dread the special pack I am now training."

I smiled.

"I shall not be afraid," I answered.

A pleased expression crossed her face.

"Then you, Mr. Druce, shall come with me. You alone. Come at once," she added, "This way, please."

We left the house and, crossing the broad avenue, went down a sloping path which led through the pine woods. As we walked I peered through the trees, and just before me a few hundred yards away I saw a cluster of low buildings or kennels which as are used to keep foxhounds in. These kennels were, however, very much stronger than those required by the master of a pack of hounds. They were of strong brick on three sides, and in front were placed high iron railings which fenced in a sort of yard. This was further divided into compartments, one compartment for each kennel, and the whole was covered over at the top with an iron penthouse. In short, the arrangements were very much on the scale employed by the Zoological gardens in London.

"Before I bought Cray Lodge, the late owner kept foxhounds," said Mrs. Bensasan. "I had the old kennels pulled down and built up again to suit my purpose. I have kept all sorts of wild beasts in them. My present fancy is for wolves. Taganrog, my large Siberian wolf, has proved to be more troublesome than any other animal I have attempted to subdue. I shall, of course, conquer him in the end, but I own that the task is difficult."

We had now reached the kennels. Mrs. Bensasan and I stood together outside the iron bars. The doors of the cages themselves were all open, and the wolves were outside in their yards; some lying down and half asleep, others moving restlessly up and down the narrow confines of their prisons. Mrs. Bensasan walked from one enclosure to the other, looking into each and telling me different stories with regard to the special wolves. At last she came to the enclosure where Taganrog was confined.

"You must watch from there," she said, pointing to the grass mound that stood a few feet away. "I am the only one who over ventures inside those doors. Taganrog fears me, although he will not as yet submit altogether to my treatment."

As she spoke she took a great key from her girdle and unlocked the gate in the center of the bars. When she got within she put up her hand in the direction of the iron roof and took down a big stock whip. At the end of the fall of the whip were wires loaded with balls of lead. I now noticed that Taganrog's kennel was closed. I had not yet seen the great wolf.

"What an awful weapon!" I said, pointing to the whip.

Her ugly mouth opened wide and she showed all her glittering white teeth.

"Not more awful than my beautiful Taganrog deserves. He is the grandest creature on earth and the most untamable. But never mind; my heart is set on effecting his moral reformation."

She laughed discordantly. There seemed to be nothing in tune about the woman. Already her personality was getting on my nerves. She gave me a glance, half of contempt, half of amusement.

"Watch me from the grass bank," she said. "You will see what will appear to you an ugly sight; but remember all the time that it is the reformation of the great Siberian wolf Taganrog, and that by-and-by all England, all Europe, will ring with his exploits and mine. It is a strange thing, Mr. Druce, but that great wolf seems part of me. Once, in some primeval age, we must have been akin."

She turned, and before I could utter a word walked to the kennel. The next instant a huge ray wolf sprang into sight. He was a beautiful creature, with long, very thick gray hair, a bushy tail, and a face which at first sight looked gentle as that of a Newfoundland dog. But when he saw Mrs. Bensasan, a rapid change came over him. He crouched in one corner, his teeth were bared, he growled audibly, and shivered in every limb. Mrs. Bensasan stood a foot away, holding her loaded whip slightly raised. She said something to the animal. He crouched as though to spring. In another instant the whip descended smartly on his loins. The blood flowed freely from the poor beast's back. A fierce and terrible expression broke from the woman's lips and raising the whip once again she lashed the animal several times unmercifully. I could not contain myself. I sprang forward to the doors of the cage.

She Lashed the Animal Several Times Unmercifully.

"Don't be so cruel," I said, "This exhibition is too horrible."

She turned at once at the sound of my voice. I noticed that her face was deadly white and covered with perspiration.

"Don't interfere," she said, in a dim low tone of fierce anger.

Then, fixing her eyes on Taganrog, she raised the whip once more with a menacing attitude and pointed to the kennel. The wolf gave her a cowed look from his bloodshot eyes and slunk to, growling as he disappeared.

Going up to the kennel she shut the bolt and made it fast. Then, returning the whip to its place, she opened the iron gates, passed through, locked them and faced me.

"When you came so near you were in danger," she said. "You did a mad thing. Taganrog was in the mood to spring at anyone. He fears me, but he would have torn you savagely even through the bars. In his moments of fear and passion, to tear anyone limb from limb would be his delight. You were foolhardy and in danger."

We were walking slowly back to the house and had gone about twenty yards when a cry, clear, full and piercing, rang on the air. It was so terrible and so absolutely unexpected that I stood still and faced Mrs. Bensasan.

"That was a cry of a woman," I said. "What is wrong?"

She smiled, and stood still as though she were listening. The cry was not repeated, but the next instant the howl for many wolves in evident hunger broke on the stillness.

"What was the other cry?" I asked.

"One of the wolves, perhaps," she answered, "or" — she shrugged her shoulders — "the ghost may really exist."

"What ghost?" Please speak, Mrs. Bensasan."

Again she shrugged her shoulders.

"There is a story extant in these parts to which, or course, I give no credence," she replied: "but the country folks say that the old vaults under the kennels are haunted. These vaults are useless now and out of repair, but they say that a madman once lived in Cray Lodge. He kept foxhounds and his wife died under mysterious circumstances. The story is that he shut her into the cellars and starved her. I do not know any particulars — the whole thing happened years ago — but the country folks will tell you if you question them, that

195

now and then her cry comes out on the midnight or evening air. I am rather pleased with the story than otherwise, for it keeps people off the vicinity of my wolves. You know of course why I asked you and Mr. Vandeleur here? Not only for the pleasure of your company, but in order that your exceedingly clever friend may discover if there are any people in the neighborhood who would dare to tamper with my special pets. It would be easy to throw them poisoned meat through the iron bars of their enclosures. A woman in my profession is surrounded by enemies. Ah! How excited my wolves are tonight! Listen to Taganrog; he is expressing his feelings."

A prolonged howl, full of misery, rang the air. We both returned in silence to the house.

"You will find the hall warm and comfortable, Mr. Druce. Ah! There is Madame Sara sitting by the fire; she is always good company. Go and talk to her. You need not begin to prepare for dinner for over an hour."

She left me and I went into the hall. Madame Sara was seated near the fire. The firelight fell on the red gold of her beautiful hair and lit up the soft complexion.

I sat down beside her.

"Will you answer a question?" I said suddenly. "Where is Miss Bensasan?"

"That secret belongs to her mother."

"But you know — I am certain you know."

"The secret belongs to Mrs. Bensasan," was Madame's reply.

She sat still, gazing into the flames that licked the great logs on the hearth. I watched her. She was as great an enigma to me as ever. Suddenly she spoke in a reflective voice.

"You are, of course, aware that Mr. Hilliers is the son of a very wealthy man?"

"I only know that he is a diamond merchant," I replied.

"And that," she answered slowly, "is sufficient. I shall have something to do with the elder Mr. Hilliers before long. He has just purchased Orion, the most marvelous diamond that Africa has produced of late years."

"I was not aware of it," I said.

She looked at me again; her blue eyes grew dark, their expression altered, a look of age crept into them—there seemed to be the knowledge of centuries in their depths.

"I have a passion for jewels," she said slowly, "for articles of virtue, for priceless unique treasures. I am collecting such. I want Orion. If that gem of gems becomes my fortunate possession it would mean the overthrow of a certain lady, the recovery of an unfortunate girl, and the final extinction of a fiend in human guise."

As she spoke she rose, gave me a slow inscrutable smile, and walked out of the hall.

By an arrangement which we both considered specially convenient Vandeleur and I had rooms each opening into the other; and when I heard my friend tap at my door just before midnight I felt a sense of relief. I opened it for him and he entered. Crossing the room he flung himself into a deep chair and looked up at me.

"You have something to say Druce. What is it?"

I replied briefly, giving him a full account of my interviews, first with Mrs. Bensasan and then with Madame Sara.

"You have had all the innings this afternoon," he said, with a smile. "That cry coming from the kennels is certainly ghastly."

The smile faded from his face; it looked sterner than I had ever seen it before. After a pause he said, gravely:

"This is our worst case. I offer my life willingly at the shrine of this mystery. Things have become intolerable; the end must be at hand. I have resolved to die or conquer in this matter."

As he spoke we both heard the cry of the wolves ringing out on the stillness of the midnight air.

"I shall examine those cellars tomorrow said Vandeleur. "Good night. I must be alone to think things over."

I did not detain him, and he left me.

At breakfast the next morning Mrs. Bensasan said:

"I am glad to be able to tell you, Mr. Druce, that Taganrog is coming to his senses. I have given him a long lesson last night and he begins to obey. He will be all right tomorrow night. In a fortnight's time he will be as meek as a lamb. He is, I consider, my greatest triumph. Mr. Vandeleur, I have already shown my pet wolf to Mr. Druce; would you like to see him?"

"I should," he answered, gently.

"I shall give Taganrog several lessons today," she continued, "and propose to give him his first almost immediately. Will you come with me now or later? He is a great beauty. Mr. Druce admires him immensely. I am proud to feel that I am his conqueror. Although he will always be ferocious to the rest of the world, he will soon be amenable to my least word or look."

Neither of us made any reply, and Rigby, who was present, rose, gave Mrs. Bensasan a peculiar glance, and left the room. I noticed for the first time that with all her fearlessness she seemed to make and exception in his favor. When her eyes met his she did not look altogether at her ease. Fearless and strong as was her nature, was it possible that she was in this man's power?

"Have you told Mr. Vandeleur about that peculiar cry which we both heard yesterday?" continued Mrs. Bensasan, turning to me. "It frightened you, did it not?"

"It certainly did," I replied.

"Knowing so little about wild beasts as you do I am not surprised at that," was her answer. "It is, I assure you, quite a common error to mistake the cry of a brute for that of a human being, for brutes have many tones in their voices, and the wolf in particular has a long gamut of sound in his larynx. Be that as it may, however, I should like you both to be satisfied. Under my kennels are three old disused cellars. Would you not like to go and search them? You will then know for yourselves whether there is any poor creature incarcerated there or not."

Vandeleur rose to his feet.

I take you at your word, Mrs. Bensasan," he said. "I should like to examine the cellars. Will you come with me Druce, or shall I go alone?"

"I will go with you," I replied.

"I am going down now to have the wolves locked into their kennels," said Mrs. Bensasan. "Will you follow me in about ten minutes' time?"

We did so. There were no keepers present, but Mrs. Bensasan stood within the enclosure of Taganrog's kennel with a smile on her face and the cruel whip in her hand. She unlocked the iron gates and invited us to enter. To my surprise I noticed that a great flagstone was raised within a couple of feet from the entrance to the enclosure and we saw a well-like opening in the ground.

"Here is a lantern," said Mrs. Bensasan, handing one to Vandeleur, "I will wait here until you return."

We went down at once in silence. We were both absolutely aware of the danger we ran. It would be easy for Mrs. Bensasan to drop the flagstone over us and to incarcerate us within, to starve out our lives. Nevertheless, I do not think we feared.

The air struck damp and chill about us. We heard the cries of the imprisoned wolves over our heads. There were three cellars, each opening into the other, but search as we would we could not see the smallest sign of any human being. Vandeleur stayed some time in the second cellar, examining it most minutely, feeling the walls, and stamping his feet on the ground in order to detect any hollow spot. At last he turned to me and said, slowly;

"Whoever cried that time yesterday has been removed. There is no use in our staying any longer."

We retraced our steps and soon found ourselves in the open air. Mrs. Bensasan's eyes were shining with intense excitement. There was a small, angry red spot on the center of each cheek.

"Well, gentleman," she said, "I hope you are satisfied?"

"Absolutely," replied Vandeleur.

She opened the gate for us and we passed through.

A minute later the excited cry of the release pack broke on our ears.

"Will you walk with me to the railway station?" asked Vandeleur.

"What!" I cried, in some amazement, "are you going to town?"

"Yes, for a few hours. I have got an idea in my mind. I am haunted by a memory; it goes back a good way, too. I want to have it confirmed; it may bear on this case. If it does I may be able to release Miss Laura, for that she is detained in most undesirable captivity I have not the slightest doubt."

"What about the robberies?" I asked. "Is there anything of the sort going on?"

"As far as I can tell, nothing. We must hurry, Druce, if I am going to catch my train."

I saw him off and returned slowly to the house. On my way back I met Gerald Hilliers. He was waiting to see me and began to talk at once on the subject nearest his heart.

Taganrog will be in control by tomorrow night," he said. "The exhibition is to take place by electric light, and

Mrs. Bensasan is having a small platform raised for us to stand on while she exhibits. She is anxious to accustom the wolves to the flare and light which must be present when she holds her public exhibitions. By the way," he added, suddenly, "I saw Madame Sara this morning and she told me that she has given you her confidence. She promised to help me, but on an impossible condition. My father will never part with Orion except for a fabulous price. The diamond is watched day and night by two men, and the safe in which it is secured is practically impregnable. There is no help whatever in that direction."

"There Is No More Hope Whatever In That Direction."

"Have you told Madame Sara yet about your father's view of the matter?" I asked.

"Yes."

"And what did she say?"

"She smiled."

"Then, Hilliers, I counsel you to beware. I like Madame least of all when she smiles."

Vandeleur returned rather late that evening. He informed me briefly that he was satisfied with his investigations, and that it was his intention to force Mrs. Bensasan's hand by means known only to himself, if she did not soon reveal her daughter's whereabouts.

The next day was Wednesday: that night we were to see Mrs. Bensasan in the hour of her triumph. I awoke with an overpowering sense of restlessness and depression. Vandeleur was seen talking earnestly with Mrs. Bensasan soon after breakfast. Their conversation was evidently of an amicable kind, for when it was over she nodded to him, smiled, and hurried off in the direction of the kennels.

Vandeleur then, with long strides, disappeared up the avenue. I wondered what he was doing and what was the matter. I wanted his confidence, but did not care to press for it.

Shortly before lunch, as I was walking on the borders of the pine wood, I was amazed to see Madame Sara drive up in a dog-cart. She saw me, pulled in the mare which she was driving herself, flung the reigns to the groom and alighted with her usual agility.

"Ah!" she called out, "I am glad to see you. You wonder where I have been."

I made no reply.

"Confess to your curiosity," she continued. "This is an extraordinary day, and my nerves are in a strange state. Much-everything-hangs on the issues of tonight. Mr. Druce, I want to confide in you."

"Don't!" I could not help exclaiming.

"You must listen. This is what has happened. When friends fall out—ah! you know the old proverb—well friends have fallen out, for Mrs. Bensasan and I have quarreled; oh, my friend, such a quarrel! A point was to be solved. Julia Bensasan wished the solution to take one form, while I was just as resolved that it should take another. She is a powerful woman, both physically and mentally, but she is destitute of tact. She has no reserve of genius in her nature. Now I --" she drew herself up---"I am Madame Sara, known to the world for very remarkable abilities. In this conflict I shall win."

"Explain, will you?" I said.

"Ah! You are curious at last, Mr. Druce, it is a very remarkable fact that you and your friend should have been fighting so hard against me for so many months, and in the end be altogether on my side."

"Need you ask?" she replied. "Are not your wishes and mine identical? We want to make a girl happy. We have resolved to give her to the man who loves her and whom she loves. Need I say more?"

"Madame Sara," I said, "you do nothing without a price. Have you a chance of receiving the diamond?"

"I have a passion," she said, slowly, "for things unique, strange, and priceless. I go far to seek them, still farther to obtain them. Neither life nor death stands in my way. Yes, the stone is mine."

"Impossible!"

"It is true I went to town this morning. I saw old Mr. Hilliers. He gave me the diamond. I keep it on a condition."

I was speechless from amazement. She looked right at me, then said slowly:

"I find the lost girl and give her to Gerald Hilliers."

"But why has his father changed his mind? Gerald told me only yesterday how callous he was with regard to the whole matter."

"Ah! He is callous no longer. He and I have both a desire. I, for unique treasures and he for unlimited wealth. The love of gold is his passion. I have informed him with regard to some things in connection with Mrs. Bensasan. She is one of the richest women in England; Laura is her only child and heiress. I have done something else for him."

"What is that?"

"Imparted to him a secret by which he can in a measure recover his lost youth. To offer a man both youth and riches presents a temptation impossible for the ordinary man to resist. Mr. Hilliers is quite ordinary; he struggled, but in the end succumbed. I knew he would."

"Will you tell me one thing?" I said. "Why does Mrs. Bensasan want her daughter to marry Joe Rigby? Is he so rich and so desirable?"

She came a step nearer.

"Your friend, Mr. Vandeleur, is on the track of that secret," she said. "I could tell him now, but I delay just for a time. As you know so much you may as well know this. Rigby is greater and more powerful than the richest man or the most beautiful or the greatest on earth. He holds a secret — it is connected with Mrs. Bensasan. Laura is the price of his silence. Ah! Have I been overheard?"

She sprang from me. There was a rustle in the bushes near by. I rushed up to them and tore them asunder. No one was to be seen. But Madame Sara's face had changed. It was full of a curious, most ghastly fear.

"I have been imprudent," she said in a low voice, "and for the first time in my life, is it possible that success has turned my brain?"

She did not wait to give me another glance, but hurried to the house.

We dined early that night, as Mrs. Bensasan's exhibition was to take place at 8 o'clock. The dinner was gay; the conversation bright; repartee and sparkled like champagne. On the face of Bensasan, however, there was a fierce, cruel look, which was so dominant that, with all her efforts to appear friendly, sociable — in fact, the perfect hostess — she utterly failed. Once her eyes fixed themselves on Madame Sara's beautiful and charming face, and the expression in their agate depths was far from good to see.

The dinner came to an end. It was too soon to go to the kennels.

"There is still time enough" remarked Mrs. Bensasan, addressing Madame Sara. "Follow me in five minutes. You an dI have our work to do first. When we are quite ready for

206

the curtain to rise and the show to begin, my keeper, Keppel, shall announce the fact to the gentlemen."

Mrs. Bensasan went slowly from the room. I had never before been so impressed. Madame Sara beside her hostess looked, slender, almost childish.

"That woman is the greatest of her age," said Madame. "How great only I who have known her for years can imagine. Mr. Rigby and I both know Mrs. Bensasan well, don't we, sir?"

None of us spoke, and she went slowly towards the door. Just as she reached it she turned and faced us.

"I have provided against possible mischief," she said.

She thrust her hand into the bosom of her dress and drew out a small revolver. Minute as it was, I knew the sort, and was well aware that it could be used with deadly effect. With a gentle and sweet smile she returned it to its place; then, taking up a cloak which lay on a chair near, she flung it over her evening dress and disappeared into the night.

Four of us were now left in the hall — Rigby, Hilliers, Vandeleur and myself.

"We shall be summoned in a minute," said Vandeleur. "This is a state of tension quite unpleasant in its strain."

He walked to the house door and threw it open. He had scarcely done so before the sharp crack of a shot sounded from the pine wood below the house. It was followed instantly by another. Fearing we knew not what, we all rushed from the hall and flew down the path through the pine wood. The bright electric light guided us: the howl of many wolves smote savagely on our ears.

In a very short time we had reached the little platform which had been erected in front of the huge cage where Mrs. Bensasan had arranged to give her exhibition. The gage was there, but to my surprise there was no keeper in sight. We instantly crowded on the platform and saw Mrs. Bensasan standing upright in the middle of the cage. She had a stock whip in her hand. A woman lay prostrate at her feet. The woman's fair hair streamed along the floor of the cage; her cloak was torn aside. There was a large and ghastly wound in her throat; blood covered the floor. At a little distance lay Taganrog, shot through the head and motionless. When she saw us approach Mrs. Bensasan turned. Her face was quite calm and her manner quiet. She looked down at the figure of the fallen woman.

"Madame Sara, the great Madame Sara, is dead," she said, with slow distinctness. "She ventured into the cage; it was imprudent—I implored her not to come, but she would not heed. Her death is due to Taganrog. He feared me, but the sight of her maddened him. He sprang at her and tore her throat. It was but the work of a second. See, I have shot him. But madame had also a revolver, and just in the moment of—of—ah! Heavens! Ah!"

She tottered; over her face there came an awful expression and the next instant she was also lying on the floor of the cage. Long quivers passed over her frame. She was evidently in mortal agony. We all rushed forward, burst open the door of the cage, and entered.

Vandeleur went on his knees and bent over the prostrate woman.

"I die," she said; "I have only few minutes to live. Listen!"

She tried to press her hand to her side; a great spurt of blood poured from her lips.

"I am shot through the lungs," she said. "Hers was the surest aim in the world. You may know all now. Madame Sara and I arranged this exhibition, and you, Mr. Vandeleur, were to be the victim. Madame got you both down her on purpose. It was she who thought the thing out; we did not believe we could manage the death of you both, but one at least seemed certain. Your methods were more deadly than those of Mr. Druce, therefore you were appointed to be the victim. But, when the wicked quarrel—ah! You see for yourselves the result. You shall know all now.

"Joe Rigby—yes, he is there, but it doesn't matter; he knew a story about me, Madame also knew, but he had the evidence, and she had not. He could hang me—it happened years ago—I poisoned my husband."

"I know," said Vandeleur. "I found the particulars yesterday in the books at Westminster. I meant to speak to you tomorrow—but no matter."

"Bah!" she said, "nothing matters now. I hated that feeble man. I poisoned him with arsenic. Rigby knew, and from that day he blackmailed me heavily. Six months ago he set his heart on securing my pretty, gentle, Laura—Laura with her money was to be his price. I did not dare to give her to another. I was determined that she should marry him; I would make her submit. One night Madame and I took her away in a cab. This was to blind the neighbors. Towards morning we brought her back and put her into the cellars below the kennels. When you, Mr.Vandeleur, examined them, you knew nothing of a small dungeon below the second cellar. Laura was put there. She is gagged in the dungeon now. You will find the spot by a jagged cross scratched over the stone above. She is uninjured. She inherits my money.

209

When I die Rigby will be powerless. You can give her to the other man."

Vandeleur placed his hand under her shoulders and slightly raised her head.

"Madame shot me through the lungs," she continued. "My life is only a matter of minutes. I go to my death unafraid. Madame, at least, is dead. She was cleverer than I and more subtle. Ah! There was never a brain like hers. She arranged to help me; Rigby should obtain Laura, and you, Mr. Vandeleur, should die. All was going well, but avarice got the better of her. For the sake of a stone, a bauble, she gave me up, and I could not brook that. I resolved that the means which were meant to compass your death should compass hers. Revenge became the strongest motive of my life. My intention was, had all succeeded, to lay the blame on Taganrog. It would have been natural, would it not, to suppose that the wolf—But look!"

Her eyes sought the floor, and Vandeleur, bending down, picked up two great sets of steel teeth, fashioned somewhat after the teeth of a wolf. They jangled horribly as he shook them in his hand. The dying eyes gleamed.

"She made them," whispered the exhausted voice. "She made them for me to use in order to take you by surprise, to spring on you and tear your throat out. An excuse was to be made which was to bring you first on the scene tonight. The keepers were to be dismissed beforehand. All the world would suppose it was an accident and that the wolf had destroyed you. She and I would have known better. I guessed her treachery and followed her today, and heard what she said to Mr. Druce. Instantly I changed my tactics. You should live, but she should die! I sent for her first on purpose. She must have scented my change of front, for she had her revolver. The wolf killed her—I had no need to use those hideous teeth; but before she died she raised that toy instrument and inflicted my death wound. It was I who shot the wolf — "

Her voice faded away into silence. The dimness of death covered her awful, too bright eyes. A minute or two later she breathed her last.

"The Great MMe. Sara Is Dead."

We rescued Laura Bensasan from her terrible prison. We took from that den a distracted and nearly mad girl. We brought her back to the house, and did all that ingenuity and kindness could suggest for her benefit. But one look at Hilliers was better for her than all our sympathy. She flew to him. He took her in his arms. He loved her and she loved him. There was no longer any bar to their happiness and future union.

The End

Made in the USA
Columbia, SC
19 August 2020

16814286R00117